17

17
A
Novel
in Prose Poems

Liz Rosenberg

Cricket Books

A Marcato Book

Chicago

Printed in the United States of America

Designed by Anthony Jacobson

First edition, 2002

Library of Congress Cataloging-in-Publication Data

Rosenberg, Liz.
  17 / Liz Rosenberg.
      p. cm.
"A Marcato book."
Summary: Seventeen-year-old Stephanie journeys from fall to spring and
from childhood to womanhood as she experiences first love and deals with
her fear of inheriting her mother's mental illness.
  ISBN 0-8126-4915-X (alk. paper)
  [1. Mental illness—Fiction. 2. Interpersonal relations—Fiction. 3.
Poetry—Fiction. 4. Family life—Massachusetts—Fiction. 5. High
schools—Fiction. 6. Schools—Fiction. 7. Massachusetts—Fiction.] I.
Title.
  PZ7.R71894 Se 2002
  [Fic]—dc21

                                                2002006454

A few of the passages in this novel first appeared, sometimes in slightly different form, as prose poems in the collection *These Happy Eyes* by Liz
Rosenberg, published by Mammoth Press, 2001.

To my husband, David, aka Mephisto,
who didn't sneer when I first called it poetry.
My love, always and from the start—

And to all the other beloveds who helped
me survive that thing called adolescence.

Deep thanks to and no blame to
Joëlle Dujardin, Judy O'Malley,
and—as ever—Marc Aronson
for their editorial efforts
and pastoral care.

LMR

17

Begin the Beguine

First day back, and a flock of coal black birds flies up and off, weaving a spiral south. They know something she doesn't. It's officially summer still, and hot as hell, but the first day of school always means fall.

Smell of new shoe leather and backpack, wet leaves, dew on the cut grass. The girl gets as far as the curb. She's a skinny seventeen, looks fourteen, is wearing clunky red leather shoes that practically match her long dark red hair. She runs back inside the sleeping house, brushes her teeth (again), washes her face (again), looks in the mirror, and tells herself to cut it out.

She sneaks one of her mother's pills from the cabinet, swallows it with a doll-size Dixie cup of faucet water, and hurries back into the sticky heat. The bus comes to ferry her off to the underworld of eleventh grade.

The Asylum

Assistant principal Mrs. Serbuck paces outside, looking left, right, forward, furiously, her head swiveling. She stands under the portico outside the school building, barking at the new arrivals. Hard to tell if she is here to greet or scare them away. She is howling about something, frothing at the mouth, but what? Half the kids aren't even off the buses yet.

Dr. Janaceck, principal, stalks back and forth, disappearing, reappearing, his mouth bitter. He greets her by name, "Stephanie," nodding disapprovingly as his lips form the three syllables.

Girls gather on the lawn, all of them in cotton flowered dresses, turning the front of the school into a wild field of flowers. Pink, yellow, rose, yellow, yellow, cobalt blue. They turn in one looping wave when another bus arrives and half the girls cry out one name, "Denny! Denny's back! Denny!"

Yellow, blue, and white blossoms. "Denny!"

Stephanie turns to see this marvel, but a figure looms up beside her as if the ground had opened beneath his feet. His hand seizes her shoulder.

His gruff voice says, half kidding, "Outta my way," and the figure roughly pushes her aside. The tall boy lopes on in black T-shirt and black jeans, a moving shadow above the grass.

"That was Denny Pistil," her friend Lisa says, as if it should mean something. But she hears the word *pistol*, so she thinks gun, not flower.

Home on the Range

Stephanie's mother is in a good mood. She rules their world with a soft fist. Stephanie's little brother—his school doesn't start till next week—flies to the front door. "Mom's been working all day."

It's like coming into a room with party lights on where you had extended a hand forward, frightened, expecting to fall into pitch darkness.

Big-boned, solid, golden blonde, larger than life, and taller than her daughter by a head, Clarissa is wearing her work clothes, old linen and cotton, soft and earth-toned even before the clay has stained them. "I've been out at the studio," she confirms.

The boy escapes, quicksilver, into the den to read his precious sci-fi novels.

"Come see what I've made," the mother says. Mother and daughter step carefully over clay pots and bowls, over figures and disembodied hands and heads.

A sculpted trio of girls holding hands. The mother has braided their hair of clay with care, a few tendrils escape. One girl's foot is lifted in midair. Another leans back, her mouth open in laughter. The serious-looking one who seems to be the leader. A smell rises deep from the earth of which they are made. The mother rests her hand near her daughter's shoulder—not on it, not wanting to get her first-day-of-school clothes dirty. "That's you," she says, nodding toward the trio.

"Which one?" the girl asks.

"All of them," Clarissa answers, smiling that igniting smile.

Day Moon

When Stephanie walks the dogs at eight at night, it's still light out, deep, shimmering September blue. The TV set comes on in the house of the Overbrooks across the way. It's a painting come to life, with moving stained-glass figures. TV colors shine through the thin white curtains. Even the dogs are eager, pulling her forward over her feet.

No hint of this morning's foolish dread. The first day of school was—just ordinary school. Same long hallways, same teachers, same library, same faces (mostly), and same dull subjects.

Above, a white crescent moon floats in the blue sky. A few stars. Everything bright as polished gems. Promising something. The faintest hint of cool weather floating in. Sometimes the girl is so happy, she doesn't know what on earth to do with herself.

At Night, Alone in Bed

No one ever talks about this. Face pressed into the pillow. She doesn't want to, not really, but she does think of a tall gaunt figure, larger than life, dressed in black, brushing against her as his strong swift muscular legs carry him downhill, toward other girls.

Afterward, she rolls on her back, and it seems sad and ridiculous never to share this sweetness with anybody else.

Morning will wash these minutes away as if they never happened.

The Hero

He's in her advanced history class, her advanced English class, her advanced science class, her unadvanced lunch block. He is friends with all of Stephanie's smart friends from the other middle school, the one on the north side, with the big brick houses and the nice mall.

He's been away the last two years—gone to school in Eton, England, where his father, specializing in international law, was . . . attorney to Her Majesty the Queen. High and exalted Rich Guy. Keeper of the Royal Treasury. At least that's the way people talk about it.

No one but the teachers ever calls him by his real name: Dennis.

Dennis Pistil.

"Denny," he corrects them, politely, but there's something chilly—he's so tall and overconfident—he never has to correct them twice. They are anxious to please; even the teachers try to impress him.

She has to go through school begging, Please call me Steph, not Stephanie. A girl who loves poetry and flowers. A typical girl. A redhead. A girl who wears flowered skirts and an overbright smile.

Denny is starting to bald prematurely. Maybe he's a grown man disguised as a teenager. When she glances at him, he's glancing at her. But they don't speak—not yet.

Keets and Yeets

Their English teacher hates poetry. Why hasn't he found another profession? He says, "All seventeen-year-olds write poetry . . . especially all the girls." One day he pronounces the Irish poet's name Yeats, so it rhymes with Keats. Yeets and Keets. Denny leans back in his chair, his mouth drops in surprise.

She cringes, sitting in view of this boy for whom public school means private school, who's going to Oxford, everybody says, whose father is rich and mighty, an Olympian. Which makes Denny the son of a god.

She feels personally responsible for their teacher's bad pronunciation, this school, the village, the township, the entire state of Massachusetts, the United States of America. After class Denny blocks her way out of the room. He stands, legs apart, taking up the doorway. She tries to smile at him, but somehow her lips fail her, and tremble, twist sideways awkwardly instead.

He says, "I hear you write poetry. I'd like to see it."

She says, "All girls write poetry."

He says, "I'd just as soon start with yours."

He says, "Tomorrow."

He says, "During lunch. In the library, tomorrow," but not

like it's a question. He turns and takes the hall in five long strides.

At Seventeen

She stands looking in the bathroom mirror. Yes, she still recognizes the child there; skinny, dark-red-haired, long nosed, pale skinned, freckled. But isn't there a new sharpness in the dark eyes? Is it anger? Is it hope?

Something else?

Her legs are growing thicker, the thighs, even though she is still flat chested and bony everywhere else. Her lips are too thin. When she smiles, her upper lip practically disappears. Her best friend Lisa says, "You are so beautiful this is just ridiculous."

She just feels ridiculous.

She stands at the edge of—a bridge, a road, a mood, a field. Wandering a little farther off. A little farther each day. But is she drawing closer, too?

And to what?

Dinner at the Homesick Café

Sister sits. Father sits. Brother sits, wriggling, kicking his legs under the table and fidgeting. Mother rushes around, clanging the pot lids like ancient musical instruments, brings in one dish at a time, running back into the kitchen. It hurts the eyes to look at her, her yellow-gold hair, her round blue eyes giving off sparks.

"I'm forgetting something," she murmurs. "Aren't I?" Then, "No, don't get up!" when anyone moves to help. Her own movements too quick, jumpy.

She's made Bizarro salad with organic greens, pimentos and chopped-up watermelon. The chicken, not completely cooked, is topped with avocado rings, topped by squares of melting cheese, topped by some kind of roasted corn compote, topped by a pink rose.

The brother, Justin, always diplomatic, says, "What the heck *is* this?"

The mother stops in her tracks. "What do you mean?"

The father says, "Your mother worked very hard to prepare this meal."

The mother says, "I know I forgot something!" and rushes wildly back to the kitchen. Father and daughter exchange glances. He is a mere mortal. His shoulders slump. He pokes at the compote with his fork and says to his son, "Eat."

"How?" asks the boy.

It is a good question. No one can answer him.

In the Basement

Clarissa is pulling canned goods off of shelves, strewing jars all over the floor. Canned corn, lima beans, green beans, baby peas. A garden's worth. She has bought ten, twenty of each kind of jam: strawberry, raspberry, apricot, cherry. "Mint jelly would be good," she says, "but now I can't remember, did I make mint jelly this summer or not?"

Her daughter doesn't think so and leads her mother upstairs, holding tightly onto her elbow. Clarissa lets herself be directed, and sits at the dinner table. "Wow, this looks terrible," the mother says miserably. "I wish we had some mint jelly."

"Mint jelly," the boy intones, "would make all the difference."
He is eight, and no one's sure how much he understands.
How much he wants them to understand.

The mother pushes back her chair. "Did I leave something boiling on the stove?"

The father puts one hand on her arm. "Sit," he says. "Please, Clarissa . . . Sit."

But Clarissa can't sit, can't be still, not for an instant. Crashing sounds from the kitchen, the basement. It will take hours to clean up. Luckily no one has homework yet.

Stephanie makes her brother an extra good lunch for the next day: a roast beef sandwich, rare, his favorite, cut in neat quarters; cherry tomatoes tied up in a baggy; a foil bag of potato sticks; two boxes of juice; and for dessert, dried apricots mixed with chocolate chips. She takes a bite out of the sandwich before wrapping it up in tinfoil. Justin likes this tradition—the father started it. The father takes bigger bites, and Justin says his sandwiches taste better. They are a matched pair, those two.

Later that night, when she tucks her brother in and smooths back his hair, he puts down the book he's reading and asks, "Are all families like ours?"

"Not all," she says.

He nods. "Some are."

Outside his window, the first star shining in the dark blue silken sky. She tells him to make a wish. He wants it to come true, and keeps it to himself.

Why Justin Was Born

Justin is nine years younger. Once she asked her mom, why did she have him?

Clarissa explained, "I guess I was just having a bad day."

Sweaty Hands

Sitting in the library, the mild stir of autumn outside the windows. The season is falling into fall. Flowers barely still alive look like they are burning up. Orange, yellow, gold. A few sumac leaves bright crimson.

It is lunch hour. She can see his head tall above, almost unmoving, two tables away, but she doesn't go to him. Her palms are sliding on the table because she is sweating, and she panics a minute, thinking, What if he comes over and wants to shake hands? She thanks God no one shakes hands anymore.

As usual, he is surrounded by other girls. He seems to have no friends who are male—just one or two pale boys who follow him around.

She tries to concentrate on a poem she is writing for English class. It takes place in spring and is flowery and dull. The teacher would definitely call this "girl poetry." She decides to take out the flowers and substitute rocks.

A cliff appears in the poem, startling her.

She is concentrating so completely on what her eraser is doing that she jumps when a hand lands on her shoulder. Holding her in place. Denny is smiling at her. "Ready?" he says.

"Okay, then." He sticks out that big hand—and she has no choice but to shake it with her own sweaty hand.

Folders

The English teacher files their poetry into folders, and instructs them to comment on the poems of four classmates.

Why four; why not two, or seven? Or twelve. She keeps her folder near the bottom of the pile, where someone would have to hunt to find it.

Denny's handwriting is spiky and left-handed. He writes in black ink on the top of one of her poems, "Beginnings are delicate things."

What It Feels Like

Like having wings on your heels, eyes in the back of your head, and those eyes are always watching, afraid even to blink, looking around. Where is he now? And now? Every nerve is straining toward something that is out there— beyond her control, so it's as if she has her body, but someone else has her soul. Everything shines. The season. The window seats, desktops, tangerine-colored school buses glowing in late afternoon sun.

Words to the dumbest songs take on new, deep meanings. She is patient and tender and irritable, snapping at everyone.

He has beautiful cloud-clear blue eyes, cloudy like sky on a beautiful rainy day. He has long hands, long fingers, long legs, and long brown hair that falls into his eyes. A long nose with a bump in it. A voice that sounds always a little as if he's catching a cold.

At home she writes his name in the steam on the glass of the shower door, then writes her name next to his.

She makes up poems about him that she would never put into the poetry folder. She dances seductively in front of the mirror and wonders what he would think of her dancing. She wears the kind of nightgowns she imagines he would find sexy. Soft white thin cotton with lace, she thinks.

Practices kissing the pillow, which never kisses back or gives her a clue what to do next. She wishes she had kissed more.

Justin and His Dad

Near midnight, the two of them read together in the den. Father and son. They take turns dipping their hands into a bowl of snacks. They eat awful things: taco chips and M&Ms and cheese-peanut-butter crackers dyed bright orange and cereal filled with marshmallow bits.

The father reads science fiction. The brother reads chapter books, mysteries, and science fiction. Justin's favorite book is *A Wrinkle in Time*. He's checked it out fourteen times from his school library.

She's offered to buy him a copy, but he says, "No, I like this one." Sometimes he reminds her of Charles Wallace, the weird little kid who goes and gets himself hypnotized by a giant brain. But Justin is the giant brain.

The father's larger hand dips into the bowl, rises slowly to his mouth, then the brother's little hand dips in and rises, the two of them working at it steadily, like a two-piston engine.

One day she says to the dad, "That little stomach is eating the same garbage your big one is," and he looks up from his book, mildly surprised.

"You're right," he says mildly. "Sorry, Just. Your sister's right. No more snacks."

But they both look so mournful at the prospect, she fills their bowls with apple slices, separates oranges and pomegranates into sections, serves them dry-roasted peanuts with organic raisins, or cups of all-fruit sherbet. It's exhausting, constantly preparing food and serving it, and clearing it afterward because no matter how much she screams and threatens, neither one of them ever remembers to move or clean a dish.

The mother is going to bed earlier each night, with the autumn sun. She used to come into the den after everyone had trotted in and out of the kitchen all night. She would announce, "Attention, attention! The kitchen is now closed!" And that was it. Everyone stayed out.

But when the girl tries it, father and brother just look up and chuckle, as if she's told a lame joke.

The Bully

Someone is writing on their poetry folders in the library, someone who isn't in their class—rumor has it he's a senior. Maybe he's deranged, or just mean.

He signs himself "Mephisto" and picks on people, like a bully on the playground: "This is garbage," on a poem by Judy Denver, a girl six feet tall since sixth grade, with squinting eyes and stooped shoulders. On Stephen

Podgorsky's love poem to the senior honors English teacher Mephisto writes, "Die, you impudent dog! Grovel in your infinite hypocrisy."

Stephanie talks to her English teacher, who shrugs. "The dogs bark, but the caravan moves on."

Everyone seems to know who this Mephisto is, but no one seems to care. Why should she?

Lisa says, "Maybe he just likes poetry. Maybe bad poetry offends him."

A thought occurs to Stephanie. "Do you know this guy? You do, don't you! Do you actually like him?" Lisa doesn't answer, but her pinched, homely face turns bright red.

Love is so strange, so unpredictable.

Suffering

When she gets home from school, the house looks as if it's been scrubbed with a toothbrush. Burned clean. Her mother is sitting with a piece of paper in front of her.

Steph can see it's a list. At first she thinks a grocery list; words are written on it in a backhand scrawl: *Doctor,*

Actress, Lawyer, Violinist, Track Star, Ophthalmologist, Mother, Architect.

"These are some of your options," the mother says.

The girl turns the page around to face her, buying time. "Ophthalmologist? Architect?"

"Why not?" Clarissa says. "You're a capable person."

"My architecture project in eighth grade," Stephanie says, "was a house in the shape of a T. You had to walk from one end to the other to get to the bathrooms. When I added snow with shaving cream, it collapsed."

Clarissa draws a line through the word *Architect.* "Okay?" she says. "Now are you happy?"

Her eyes are ultrabright blue, swimming-pool blue, and she's whipping the pencil up and down between her fingers so it looks like the blur of a hummingbird, hitting the table *bang-bang-bang.* "I want you to realize your potential. I don't want you to forget women are—women are . . . I'm going downhill again," she adds. "I feel it coming. One minute it's so beautiful, the scenery is rushing by, and the next you're going ninety-six-billion miles an hour with the sun rushing straight at your nose, and your foot is stuck to the gas pedal. No matter what, you're going to crash."

"We should really call Dr. Davin," her daughter says.

"No," the mother says. "No hell no. Lithium turns me into a zombie. I just need some rest. Would it be all right if I take a nap? I made a list for Justin. Make sure you go over it with him, all right?"

"I will," the girl says. On the back of her piece of paper is another list, with Justin's name at the top and words like *"Bird watcher, Pelican, Penguin, Poet, Politician"* and other things totally illegible. Clarissa must have finished the girl's before she started on Justin's.

The girl pulls the flowered duvet coverlet over her mother. How many countless times has she crawled into bed and lain there, watching her sleep? How many mornings and afternoons? Sometimes the mother needs the room dark. Sometimes she sleeps with the lights on. The old safe days of cuddling, mother and daughter.

Once, in grade school, when she was asked to write down her mother's hobbies, she had written, "Napping."

"Just leave it," Clarissa says, and puts one arm over her eyes, blocking everything out. It's a pitiful, heroic gesture.

If the girl could sculpt the way her mother does, she would sculpt her right now, and call it "Suffering."

The Lucky Few

Denny writes long formal comments about her poems, closely written, scrawly black ink, both sides of the paper. He lists the poets she should be reading—Auden, Wallace Stevens, Dylan Thomas, Marianne Moore—schools of criticism and techniques she ought to try.

The whole thing is as impersonal as a letter from the bank till the last paragraph. "I won't try to analyze the meaning of these, but will leave that to the few—the lucky, lucky few—who know you well."

The lucky few. She could throw herself into his arms. She smiles radiantly every time she sees his dark figure stalking the halls, as if he had plucked her up apart from all the others, kept for himself. The very lucky few. Only later, when she knows him well, will she realize this was his idea of a joke.

Friends

She's never had a close friend who was a boy.

She's never been close to any boy except her little brother, Justin, not after fifth grade when it began to mean something different.

But Denny's girl friends are friends who happen to be girls. That's what he says, and what they say. All the same, they give her funny looks, as if they are studying her to figure out something improbable if true.

She's not sure if that's how it always is with friends. Lisa doesn't seem to know, either. She wishes she had more friends of either sex so she could ask.

The Moon

She's shaken awake, one hand on her shoulder. The room is pitch dark; the clock reads 2:12. "Come on," Clarissa says. Her voice is eager and wide awake. "Come on, it's wonderful!"

"No," Stephanie groans, turning over in the bed and wrapping herself like a mummy. This has happened too many times, too many middle-of-the-nights. "Go away."

But Justin is there, too. "Come on, Steph," he says. "It's cool. Really. . . . It's a lunar eclipse," he says. "Come on." The urgency in his voice pulls her out of bed. Maybe he's truly excited about this eclipse, or just afraid to disappoint his mother, but she goes. She stands barefooted in a baggy T-shirt and pajama bottoms, and follows them without a word up to the roof.

It's a flat roof at the back of the house, with a view of fields and the Berkshire Mountains beyond. Their father is already there, in an old paisley robe. He is watching something through their not-very-expensive telescope.

The moon, about three-quarters full, looks covered over with white tissue paper. The tissue seems to be shredding; the real moon is shining through. Then it's as if a hand takes all that away and pulls a veil tight. She sucks in her breath. Behind it, the moon shines like an opal. It flashes fire, then goes dead; grayish black.

She wants to rush downstairs and call Denny, but of course it's much too late and, strangely enough, they've never even talked on the phone.

Her mother stands with her arms close around her. Clarissa surveys the field calmly as if she owned every inch of it, as if she had summoned it. There has never been any place safer than her mother's arms. They are an affectionate family, always hugging and snuggling. But this, this is home. This is where she feels safest.

Now the moon looks dull silver, like a mirror when someone breathes on it. . . . Maybe it will always be that way, the rules of nature undone. The girl shivers and her mother's arms tighten just a little. Justin and her father are murmuring softly together, pointing out constellations and planets. The father is explaining something about physics.

Her mother's arms are around her like a cloak against the cool of the night. "My baby girl," Clarissa says. It makes her feel safe, but it's hard to breathe. She wishes she could be looking through the telescope, breathing the night air.

First Things

Everything green is turning brown, and a freakishly early light snow begins to fall. She wonders if Denny wants to go inside, but he seems content to keep on walking, steadily, with the first flakes landing on his hair and on the shoulders of his jacket. Even the snow clings to him. Frosts his hair silvery white.

They cross a small creek that runs through the back of the soccer field. He puts one gloved hand out to help her cross. At the touch of the cold leather against her fingers, she shudders, like a small animal, and hopes he doesn't notice.

They walk in absolute silence, and when it seems impossible to go any further without saying something, he stops. Takes off his glasses, which leaves his face looking younger, stranger, and more vulnerable. Folds them and puts them into his jacket pocket. He takes her hands in his. They are both trembling. She knows what's coming next, but feels herself falling, tumbling into the next instant, slow motion, watching herself.

The most surprising thing isn't that he kisses her but that he opens his mouth when he kisses. His tongue moves against hers, cool, wet, and probing. She thinks, in a startled voice she can nearly hear herself say aloud, "Oh! This is French kissing."

It is one thing to read about or even watch people do it in the movies, and another thing to be inside a body that another body is suddenly inside of. Her heart is slamming against his. His chilly hands slide to the small of her back. Her feet seem to be sinking into the snow, into the wet ground below the snow.

Now he stops, pulls his face back far enough to look at her.

His eyes dazzle her. They are so blue and faraway, so crystalline and myopic. She falls into a trance looking into his eyes unmasked by glasses. She barely recognizes him. He has a naked face, a kissed face. He blinks away snow. One kiss seems to be as much as either one of them can bear. Holding hands tightly, they hurry back to the warmth and light of the school.

All Day

All day she tastes his lips and breathes in the dark, musty old smell of his wool jacket. Every time she looks outside a classroom window and sees this early October snow still falling, she feels it all over again, as if the snow is falling, and she is falling into his arms, the whole world is falling, and she's being kissed, over and over.

Lisa leans over the desk and knocks her on the knee. "What on earth is the matter with you?" she says. "What is so charming about geometry?"

O Brave New World

They are reading *The Tempest* in English class, thank God, instead of *Romeo and Juliet* for the third time.

Miranda sees the sailors, young men washed up onshore. "O brave new world / That has such people in't."

"Okay, folks," says the English teacher. "What does Miranda mean by this?"

There's the usual response: the silence of the dead.

"People. Listen up, people," the teacher intones. No one says a word. She turns her head slightly. Denny is passing a note to Jeanette Hatch. Jeanette will be valedictorian. This was decided back in kindergarten. Since Jeanette is essentially genderless, Stephanie doesn't feel jealous. What she does feel is wonder and envy that Denny can find anything to say to her. Two words to rub together. "How are your grades, Jeanette? Still straight As? Keep up the good work."

No one in class moves a muscle.

"Class participation is 30 percent of your grade," the teacher reminds the graveyard. This sets off a flurry of responses.

"The sailors remind me of the creatures from the Black Lagoon," says Brian Tooney, who never reads anything that isn't either sci-fi or fantasy.

Melissa Schwartz raises her hand. She looks worried. "Which one is Miranda, Mr. Kutz? I forget."

Lorelle Frushkin decides it is time to be politically correct. "This is how the Native Americans felt when the whites first came to this country to wreck everything."

"Okay . . . good," says the teacher, which is what he would say if Lorelle said everyone in the play was an axe murderer. "Remember that Miranda has led an isolated, protected life."

"They're young men," Stephanie says, surprising herself by the sound of her own voice. She tries never to talk in class. "Maybe that's why they're beautiful to her. She's never seen any man except her father, and I mean— maybe—" Her voice gets slower and slower. Denny is looking at her. She blushes.

"Young men are definitely not beautiful," says Amanda Mullen, who definitely is. "Trust me."

But the most beautiful one of them all—the tall boy with a mop of dark hair and a big hooked nose and cool blue eyes—says, "I agree with Steph." O brave new world that has such people in't!

Things

The mother buys things. This is her new vocation. She comes home from the drugstore, where she's gone to buy aspirin, comes home with four enormous plastic bags filled with barrettes she can give away as gifts next Christmas, and twelve new lipsticks she'll never open, and packages of the wrong kind of cookies for Justin, and boxes of hair color, and enough wrapping paper for all year round: pumpkin gift-wrap paper for Halloween, papers with red poppies and Happy Birthday! scrawled in purple, and sixteen packets of tissue paper, assorted colors, because they were two for a dollar. She buys rolls of film and a new camera. She buys one hundred and twenty plastic hangers on sale.

When she walks in the door, there's a look of terror on her face because there's no place to put it all, so she throws the bags into the front closet, or into the back of her bedroom closet, where in a few weeks or months she might find it, dust clinging to the plastic, and hopefully the receipt still inside. Maybe even something she can still use. For the dark days ahead. The long, slow days.

But never any aspirin.

If Only

If only his long legs weren't so beautiful.
If only his blue eyes didn't cloud over.
If she could ignore her own yearning.
If her fingertips didn't tremble just lightly to touch him.
If only she didn't feel in the sick pit of her stomach that she was betraying—betraying what?—the world of her mother, the untouched, unscathed world of her self.
If.

Playing with Justin

"We'll do anything you like," Steph tells Justin. Being in love makes her generous.

It's hot, searingly bright—an Indian summer day, no trace of that snowy kiss a few weeks ago except deep inside.

"Anything?" Justin echoes. "Can we ride a bike?"

He's been trying, unsuccessfully, to learn how to ride since he was five. He kept his training wheels on till that past summer, when the other kids began to torment him.

She rigs him up for safety: knee pads, heavy jeans, finger-less gloves for grip, the helmet, which is still just slightly too big for his head so that his skull seems to wobble on his neck like a flying saucer. "Ready?"

He nods.

She trots along beside him, keeping one hand on the bike. "Don't let go!" he hollers. "Don't let go!"

"I'm not letting go." Luckily, she's a fast runner and he's a slow rider. He wobbles every time he gets near a corner, braking and curving dangerously to one side, so she has to practically carry the bike upright to keep it from falling over.

"Don't let go!"

"I'm not!" she says. "See?"

She's got one hand on one handlebar, not holding the whole thing up anymore.

"Don't let go!" he yells in his husky voice. "You don't want me to die, right?"

"Right," she says. "Now I'm going to keep holding on, but you're not going to feel it. I'm going to run along behind you."

He twists his head so far he almost swivels the whole bike around. She has to grab it, then runs behind the bike again. He's afraid to turn around and look. She can see the little wing insignia on the backs of his special sneakers, the ones he begged their mother to buy for him. As if it would make him the flying boy of his dreams.

"You're holding on!" he calls to her. "You're holding on, Steph, right?"

"Right!" she says. "There you go!"

He must hear that her voice is several yards behind him now but he doesn't seem to care, and she watches him pull farther and farther away, his short legs pumping hard. "What are you holding on with?" he cries.

"Never mind! I'm holding on. I'm holding on with my magic hand!"

"Great!" he calls. His voice gets farther away, and he turns the next corner, out of her sight.

She hears a muffled crashing sound, then his voice, saying, "Cripes!" and "Criminy!" Justin swore like a sailor back in kindergarten, so they taught him substitute exclamations. Now he talks like an old lady.

He's holding his hands up in the air, he's standing, checking himself all over. "It's all right," he says reassuringly, holding up both hands. "It's all right, I'm still alive!"

He is smiling now. "And I did it, Steph. Even if Mom wasn't here to watch me."

Even so.

In the Flesh

"There he is," Lisa mumbles one day in the library.

She may be practicing ventriloquism. She barely moves her lips.

"There who is?" Stephanie asks.

"Shh." Lisa shoots her a look of pure panic and moves her eyes toward a table in the corner. A hulking blond figure bends over a library desk.

Mephisto.

It looks as if he's about to explode from his ill-fitting clothes. His sweater is too tight. His pants are too short and clutch at his ankles. His shoulders are enormous; they bend like a giant's, like Atlas's, as if he has been holding up the earth too long. He seems to be all muscle and flesh.

Then he glances up. His eyes are clear light gray, like a child's, with a vacant expression. His nose looks like a boxer's, slightly squashed; his lips are full. He looks like a movie star who is popular just now—but not, just the way he looks almost handsome but definitely not.

He nods to Lisa, his cold eyes barely flickering recognition, then bends to his task again.

"What's his name?" Stephanie asks. "Has he got a real name?"

"Ben something. Please don't make a scene."

"He's the one who's been making scenes. Bullying Stephen Podgorsky, for goodness sakes."

"Don't talk to him." Lisa's hand shoots out and grips her friend's hard. "Please don't." She looks genuinely frightened.

"Is he dangerous?" He looks capable of it. Dangerous and mean. "Maybe we should report him."

"No." Lisa seems near tears. "Just leave it alone, all right, Steph? Please?"

"I promise."

But it gives her a creepy feeling, and when she looks toward his corner he is looking at them again, with a blank unreadable expression.

Her (Brief) Life as an Artist

They'd go out to her mother's studio and she'd get handfuls of clay slip to play with—cool and slick, smelling like caves and cement and the earth where earthworms live.

They sat at the kitchen table together and drew the same things together—a vase of pussy willows, the salt and pepper shakers, birds outside the window. It felt as if they had one pair of eyes, one head, one heart.

The feel of wet finger paint under her fingers, swirls of colors. She hoarded the wild pinkish magenta crayon and the soft bluish purple periwinkle in the big sixty-four-color box. She saved them for special occasions, even though her mother said they could always buy more.

Then, without anyone knowing how or why, the pictures in the girl's head, and what her hand could do about them, grew further and further apart. Her hand was a riderless horse.

One day, when she was twelve, she put down the Magic Marker she was using and said,

"I'm done."

Favorite Poems

Denny is in love with Dylan Thomas. First he gives her an illustrated version of "A Child's Christmas in Wales," and then a mailable miniature version with a thick blue envelope, then a recording of Thomas reading it, in his musical Welsh voice, warbling chant.

Finally Denny shows her one of his own poems. It is about a girl with "bay-bronze hair," by the "dolphin-gong-ringing sea. A girl mad as birds."

"This sounds a lot like Dylan Thomas," she says.

"It's better than sounding like Sylvia Plath," he says in an offended voice. "The others were rather fond of it, actually." When he's upset, he sometimes retreats to a British accent. She doesn't ask who "the others" are. She is outnumbered, outvoted, outclassed.

"I just wondered if you were deliberately modeling yourself on him," she says. "You know—as a technique."

"Well, yes," he says. "But I'd like to think I've put a bit of myself in there, too."

She keeps her eyes on the page. No matter how many times she reads the words, it doesn't feel like anything. Even his presence, looming beside her, self-possessed and judgmental, seems to create a draft in the room. A cold hollowness in her throat. She thinks this is supposed to be a love poem, but it feels like a conglomeration of words. Something else is worrying her.

"Can I ask you something?" she says.

"Naturally." His voice is big.

Hers is small. "The girl mad as birds—"

He smiles at her. He puts his hand on her hand. Her heart sinks. It flutters there, the heart of a mad girl, beating its wings against a cage.

Who's Coming to Dinner

Her mother tells her to invite Denny to dinner, but Stephanie avoids it as long as she can. She's watching closely the roller-coaster mood of the house. First wakeful, a waterfall of energy, then sleeping all the time. Mysterious packages no longer arrive at the door. Her mother begins returning things to the stores. Her footsteps no longer light and quick, she trudges over the earth.

Finally comes a week when things seem almost normal. Clarissa is around and awake when Justin gets home from school, she makes fried chicken and plays jazz during dinner and doesn't try to get up and dance to it, or burst into tears and escape to her room. So when she asks again about Denny and inviting him to dinner, the girl says okay, maybe. Soon.

"Oh goody," says Justin nastily. "I adore company."

"Denny isn't company," the father says. "He's Stephie's friend."

"Her special friend," Justin says. "He's special. . . . I'm special too." Justin is the only one who has met Denny so far, and he's not impressed. He has Scorpio moon, a jealous moon.

"Of course you're special," the father says.

"What don't you like about him?" she asks Justin.

"He's a pig monkey," Justin says, as if that explains it all.

"No, really," she insists. "What?"

"He's fruity," Justin says, reaching for dessert.

"Justin!" says the mother, shocked. She shoots her daughter a worried glance.

"He's a fruity little pig monkey," Justin says calmly. "He's fruity-tooty and he's snooty."

To everyone's surprise, including her own, Steph laughs.

Alone in the House

She and Denny are alone in the house, but Justin will be home in half an hour, and her mom's left a note saying she's running an errand and will be back soon.

They are alone in the house. Back soon, she keeps thinking, how soon is soon? and even though she's in Denny's arms and he's looking at her with that faraway cloud-crystal gaze, some part of her body keeps jerking at every noise. Now? Back now? Her heart is pounding, but not in a good way. More in an I'm-about-to-throw-up way, and she thinks, Well, isn't that romantic?

"What's wrong?" Denny says. "Am I going too fast?"

She doesn't know where he's going. Is she supposed to go with him?

She's dressed ridiculously—overalls and a plaid flannel shirt, what could be less sexy—but Denny doesn't seem to care. His mouth and his hands are all over her. She's in a panicky daze, listening for car doors, listening for her mother's footsteps, her brother's; wondering if some neighbor is going to choose this minute to come by and peer in the front window, or the postal deliverer, the UPS guy. Find them sprawled out on the living-room floor, tangled in each other's arms.

It's not easy to get the buckles of her overalls unfastened, but Denny is indefatigable. His long, thin fingers are trembling. She stops being terrified just long enough to kiss the backs of his hands. She chafes his hands between hers. His skin is always cold.

She helps him unhook the overall straps, but now there are all those little buttons on her flannel shirt, and her mother will be home before he can unbutton and rebutton them, and anyway she knows that what's underneath it is not all that different, just a little swelling for each tiny breast.

This is why she reaches one hand up to stop Denny's hand from going any further. She tells him, "It's really not worth it."

He sits up then and looks at her, frowns, looks her full in the face. "What do you mean?" he says. "You're beautiful."

"But I'm not very— I'm not . . . too developed, yet."

"I don't care," he says, and scoops her up and actually carries her, overall straps dangling, down six stairs to the rec room. It feels almost safe there in the den, where it's darker and cooler, and not in plain sight of the living-room window.

But she doesn't stay relaxed long. He takes her hand and guides it where he wants it to go, and if she tries to move her hand away even one inch, he grabs it and moves it back. His eyes are closed and he's breathing hard. This isn't romantic, it's just strange, and the air around them feels as if it's about to thunder and lightning.

She wants to get this over with and scramble back into her clothes and go upstairs, where it is safe and bright and everyday.

She keeps rubbing her hand on him back and forth, back and forth, with his hand pressing hard on top of hers, showing her how, and their mouths clinging together, and after a few minutes, not long at all, his eyes suddenly fly open and the blue of the iris is dazzling, tiny fireworks of dark blue against light blue, and he moans, his eyelashes flutter, his whole body tenses, and then relaxes.

She looks at him in amazement, as if she's just given birth to something.

His eyelids close again.

"Are you okay?" she asks.

"Sure," he says. He opens his eyes and looks around. He laughs a little, embarrassed. "A bit of a mess, but I'm fine—well, better than fine." He reaches over the coffee table, takes out a tissue and dabs at himself.

Just then they both hear the sound of a door closing upstairs, and quick light footsteps, and Justin calling, "Hey! Steph? Are you home?"

She stuffs her shirt inside the bib of her overalls, frantically, praying one or two buttons will hold it together. She buckles the straps so fast she could win some kind of buckling contest.

Denny runs his hands through his hair, adjusts his pants somehow, and stands up, unfolding his long legs, which just a minute ago were sprawled out in front of him, trembling violently.

He pulls her to her feet. When Justin comes downstairs and finds them, that's how they are—standing side by side, like two soldiers at attention, his sister looking dazed, and Denny grinning softly. Justin looks from one to the other. They don't look at each other.

"Well, okay," Justin says, as if he's closing a conversation. "Didn't you hear me knocking?" He shakes his head and walks away, upstairs. "I guess love makes you deaf *and* dumb."

Denny's Father

Denny tells her that his famous, rich, and powerful father is a drunk. His voice is stiff and formal, explaining this, as if he's giving a lecture. He looks up at the ceiling. Not at her.

"Not a drunk, actually—an alcoholic. And he's working hard on getting better. He's taking medication for it." Still watching the ceiling. She looks up. Nope, nothing up there.

"If he takes this while he's drinking, he'll get awfully sick. Really, seriously sick. And my mother will divorce him."

"Strong incentives," she says.

"Rather." He smiles grimly.

Scared

Why is she afraid? When she walks next to Denny in the halls, he's so tall, his footsteps are so far apart and fast, she feels like a mouse, scuttling to keep up. His bigness makes her smaller.

Melissa Schwartz touched her on the shoulder last week and she practically flew into the air. "What is the matter with you?" Melissa said.

She wanted to say, "I'm in love."

But is being in love supposed to make you feel like a character in a horror movie?

Meeting Kit

Diane Eisenstein is one of the few among Denny's friends who actually seems to like Stephanie. Diane was twelve when her mother died, and she looks pale and fragile, stricken still, with blue eyes almost as nearsighted as Denny's, and a small mouth. Everything about her is delicate and brilliant.

Diane wears her long, thick brown hair up but it falls down in pieces and wisps around her face. You can tell the time of day by how much of her hair is up or down. Stephanie thinks she is the most beautiful girl she has ever seen. She wishes her mother could meet her; Diane already looks like a painting, or a piece of antique sculpture.

Some boy named Kit—Diane's boyfriend, and one of Denny's best friends from their old school—lives in Wellfleet, in a large house overlooking the water. They all go together. It looks like a servant would answer the door, but Kit himself greets them, in tennis whites, thin and somehow dwarfish.

He greets Stephanie with a look of such unexpected, pure hatred it shocks her—she actually takes a step backward, but Denny grabs her arm and hauls her into the house.

Diane is even quieter than usual, as if she's been turned into stone. Kit gives them a tour of the house—which means he walks Denny through all the rooms, while she and Diane trail behind. She has a strong impulse to grab Diane's hand and run. Who would even notice? Kit never glances back, though Denny throws them a few friendly and helpless looks.

You can tell a lot about people, Stephanie believes, by what they hang on their walls. Kit's family likes abstracts in white frames. There are no pictures of living things anywhere. They have a small Rothko in the upstairs hall, with lush greens and blues fanning out like butterfly wings— but that was probably a mistake. All the other paintings are pale and geometric, with blank space around them.

Kit has his own music room. He owns a grand piano, a silver French horn, a violin and cello. Diane whispers that he plays them all, is a kind of prodigy. Steph is surprised. She cannot imagine music issuing from that unsmiling mouth.

Then the tour is over. A servant does appear at this point, serving lemonade and cookies. Kit still avoids looking at her. He goes on talking to Denny about his music—he wants to be a conductor one day. Maybe he'll be a good one, too, because when he abruptly says to Diane, "Come with me," she goes at once. Stephanie and Denny sit waiting for them to come back. They wait for twenty minutes ... thirty ... forty.

She says, Where on earth did they go? and Denny, looking uncomfortable, says, You know.

She doesn't know. Then she does. "Oh."

"Let's take a walk," she says. It's airless inside the house. It is like the inside of a refrigerator, with similar lighting effects.

They walk through a series of autumn gardens—a garden of mums, then asters, rows of purplish blue hydrangea, then a rose garden, with the last of November's red roses reaching like flames through an arched trellis. Denny holds her hands and rubs them between his own chilly hands to warm them. An apology without words. She feels strangely sad and lost. This is when they should begin feeling closer and closer, but instead it is as if each is on a different train, drawing apart, heading for a different destination.

Sometimes she worries, does she only like him because she feels she will never know him?

They come to a sunny gazebo. At least it's sunny if you perch on the railing, which is built of thick gray cedar and strong enough to support their weight. They rest their feet on the benches, and Denny leans over and kisses her. He holds her whole face in one hand. He opens his mouth and seems to be taking her in, pulling her hard into his body. He kisses her more roughly than he ever has before, as if he thinks she's stronger or tougher than she is.

Then he pulls his face away and says, "Do you think we're ready to sleep together?"

She wants to say, You're kidding, right? Instead she asks, "Have you ever?"

He barely hesitates. "With one girl, over the summer. We were quite close, actually."

She has to hang on to the wooden posts of the gazebo to keep from falling off backward. "Are you still? Quite close?" She thought he had always been alone, unattached. More like her.

"We're just friends now," he says impatiently. "What did you think?"

"What was she like?" she asks. Meaning—what did she look like, did you like her more than you like me, were you happier together, was it less cold than this?

"She was lovely," he says. "She still is. But she and I are just friends now . . . honest."

They lean toward each other. Kit calls Denny's name. The visit is over.

Kit has not said one sentence to her, not, Pleased to meet you, not even, Hello, and by the time they leave, she's given up hope that he ever will.

She hears him murmur to Denny, as a parting shot, "Well, she's no Anna."

Anna, she thinks. A lovely name. Now she knows the name of Denny's first love.

His Laughter

Is a slow, sizzling sound. It is tentative and nasal, like his voice, rumbling underground, and sometimes he actually breaks loose and makes a high sound that sounds like *hee hee hee* exploding from his somber, grown-up-looking face, as if against his will. She'll gladly make a fool of herself to make him laugh, to see a young man's lightness lift him.

But he never laughs very loud.

And he never laughs for very long.

His Eyes

When he feels sad, they darken. And when she touches him a certain way, but especially when he lets go of himself, his eyes get bright and milky, they are dazzling, and sometimes, for no reason she can understand, he starts to cry.

He holds up one big hand. "I'm not crying," he says. "I'm just trying to catch my breath."

But she has already caught the tears in the palm of her hand.

Don't Touch Me

Don't touch me, she thinks, while they are lying face-to-face in her bedroom. It's night; her parents have taken

Justin out to a kid movie. She is terrified. Maybe this is her way of being crazy like her mother.

Don't touch me, she thinks, and then, *No, there. Touch me there. Like that, don't, please please don't. Like that.*

The space heater goes on in her room, with a low roar, like an animal, and they're bathed in its red glow. His legs are so long, and his white jockeys gleam in the dark.

He's touching her, stroking her through her overalls, which are so thick you'd think she wouldn't feel anything, but instead her nerve endings feel like lit matches being struck, one after another. *Don't,* she thinks, talking to herself inside her head, warning herself, *Don't go . . . don't let go.*

She reaches her hand inside the waistband of his jockey underpants, where the skin is so smooth and so tight at the same time, and everything she touches feels strange and new. He smells musty and milky.

She's rushing into a deep, foreign place where nothing else matters. She's not in control, she's riding, galloping on a horse, he is the one steering the heat between her legs. It's just a few inches of her, but it feels like every nerve and sinew and cell are alive and crashing.

She's still not used to his man's body. She has only seen Justin's little-boy body, with its little-boy erections. Not like this otherness.

He stops. "Like this?"

The stopping is what does it.

She presses her open mouth against his for answer, and rubs up against him, bucking her hips as if someone else is doing it, jerkily, riding his hand hard. She takes the fingers of his other hand, which are curled near her face, and puts them in her mouth.

He moans, and she moans, thinking, *We sound ridiculous,* thankful it's too dark to see herself doing this, and then his fingers move fast enough to rub sparks from the blackness and she's not keeping track. She's lost inside a dark inner space where the two of them are flying out-ward, together and apart, and next thing you know they're hugging.

His hugging is a grateful hugging, but hers is a desperate clinging, hanging on for dear life. She feels sick to her stomach. She wonders absurdly, wildly, if she is pregnant.

She's too scared and sick to think straight. "Excuse me," she says politely, and she practically falls out of her bed and tumbles down the hall to the bathroom.

The toilet bowl looks like an enormous white skull. She peers down into it, the water moving just a little from bumping into it, then steadying again.

"Are you okay?" she hears Denny calling from her room. Just a few yards down the hall. It seems so far away. Another world. He sounds forlorn.

She thinks, The poor guy, and wipes her mouth with a tissue, then wets a washcloth, and runs it all over her face. It smells sour but familiar.

She should have run the faucet so he couldn't hear her. Her stomach feels clenched, tight as a fist, as if it's not done with her, not by a long shot.

She takes one of her mother's yellow pills and brushes her teeth before she walks back into the bedroom, straightening her clothes, trying to look cheerful. But she'd forgotten how dark it is in there, and her face is swallowed up in darkness.

He pulls her head close to his chest and strokes her hair.

"I'm so sorry." He sounds as frightened as she feels.

"No," she says. "It isn't you." He keeps stroking her hair. She feels regret in his cool touch. "You didn't do anything wrong. Not a bit."

She wants to say, "I can't help being crazy; it's in the blood. Run for your life!" But she doesn't say anything, just shivers in his arms.

The heater comes on, goes off again, comes on again with its roar, and by its red, glowing coils she sees that Denny is already asleep, his face peaceful as death, his mouth open so slightly there is just a thin rectangle of black between his lips.

Guilt

She wants to feel what it is to be hungry again, to open the refrigerator, look inside, and nod as if to a friend at the food in there. But her body won't let her.

It says, want one thing at a time. If you choose this body, we're going to have to starve you out. It says, pick your poison. She weighs less than a hundred pounds.

When Denny touches her these days, he turns into a creature she cannot recognize; his face sharpens. When she touches him, he makes hard little scrabbling motions with his hands in her hair. A wolf.

Her body consumes itself. It won't let her stay in the room, because then she would only be in one place, and stuck there. So her mind is always wandering away; she's listening for sounds from other rooms, the street, the world above.

If she could stop eating completely—then she'd be a slant of light under the door. She could make good her escape. Her body would turn back into a child, a baby, a seed sleeping under the ground.

Was is worth it, she wonders. The exchange of this new hunger for the old? There are times when she would give anything—anything at all—just to eat a sandwich again the way Justin does, like an innocent child.

Dark Tunnel of the Mother's Bedroom

She goes to find her mother.

Clarissa is lying in bed with the covers pulled over her shoulders and neck, one hand holding on to the edge of the blanket, as if about to pull it over her head. The blinds are drawn and closed.

Stephanie can barely make out the big creamy-looking silk roses her mother keeps in the bedroom in a copper planter, or the paintings on the walls, which are mostly landscapes and a Burliuk oil of a peasant girl holding a red bird but could be anything in this gloom, shadow paintings in a cave.

"Are you awake?" the daughter asks.

"Sleepy," she says. "Let me sleep."

"Okay," the girl says. "I'll take care of Justin. Don't worry."

"Sleep," Clarissa mumbles.

The daughter turns and gropes toward the door. The bedroom feels at least fifteen degrees cooler than the rest of the house. When she walks out into the hall, the slant of late November afternoon light coming between the bottom of a hall curtain and the sill practically blinds her, as if she's emerged from a movie theater on a summer afternoon.

Walking Around

What is she supposed to do with this bowling ball trapped inside her rib cage? She finds herself bent over with the weight of her own misery, hunched like an old woman hobbling down the halls at school, grimacing. The strange thing is, people think she's smiling. The rabid vice principal snaps, "What's the joke?" The lunch monitor asks sullenly what she is so cheery about. Her face is stuck in a grimace.

Sometimes she presses one fist against the center of her chest, to keep this thing inside. Sometimes she catches sight of herself in a pane of glass—unwashed, her hair like a fire gone out of control, too skinny, ghastly, old before her time—and thinks, Who is that?

She calls Lisa, but Lisa is involved with the school literary magazine, the editor of which is, incredibly enough, Mephisto.

"Wow," she says. "Edited by chain saw."

Lisa is silent.

"Maybe I could come to a meeting sometime," Stephanie

offers, though she really doesn't want to and can't imagine summoning up the strength to make the effort.

"What was I supposed to do while you were off with your new buddies?" Lisa says. *The King* is what she calls Denny. The Court is what she calls his friends and followers. "Take up knitting? Join a nunnery?"

Joining a nunnery sounds like a good idea. If only she were the right religion.

Pregnant

She can't stop thinking she is pregnant. She knows how unlikely it is, she's been taking health class for ten years, she knows Denny was nowhere near her, really, but she's scared all the same. And all the time.

She sees babies everywhere, on the street, in all the commercials on TV. Strollers. Articles about teenage pregnancies. On the rise in her part of Massachusetts. On the rise among the educated middle class. She frets, bargains, prays for her period to come but it's still weeks away, even if it comes on time, which it doesn't always.

She can't think about anything else, and when she does, for a little while, for even just a minute, it's as if the magnetic needle on a compass keeps pulling back to true north, and no matter how hard she pushes it away, it always edges back to the same thought. *What if I'm pregnant?*

Sometimes she thinks her heart is going to leap straight out of her chest with fright. Would the baby look like her? Like Denny? She pictures a newborn frowning, chiding her for changing his diaper the wrong way. "I'm quite uncomfortable, actually."

In social studies Mr. Wakish, her ancient teacher, asks a question and she can't come up with the answer. Not any answer. Her mouth hangs open, slack. She suddenly thinks she remembers hearing that sperm can travel outside the body, then enter. Gotcha! "I'm sorry," she says. Mr. Wakish asks her to please stay and talk with him after school.

Mr. Wakish is an old eccentric, very enthusiastic about the Civil War. To put it mildly. She had him for American history back in eighth grade, when he taught at the middle school. At the end of that year, in May, they went on a class trip to Gettysburg, Pennsylvania. He knew everyone in town: the nice woman selling Civil War bullets at Wogan's Antiques, waitresses at the Lincoln Diner, the manager at Pickett's Buffet. Now he's teaching in the high school and sometimes he looks lost with the older kids, the tough boys a foot taller. She thinks he liked it better when they were all children.

No matter what they are supposed to be covering—this year it is world cultures and history—Mr. Wakish always works it back around to the Civil War. He knows a lot of those war speeches by heart, and he's fond of reciting them.

Mr. Wakish has a long pointed white beard and long white hair—like photos of General Custer. Something goat-like about him. She once saw him chase a boy down the hall. He was surprisingly nimble. He actually caught the kid, which shocked all of them, the boy especially. Mr. Wakish almost never yells, except about the Civil War, when he is very excited about some battle or infantry unit.

"Are you having a problem, Stephanie?" he asks as she steps into his room after the final buzzer of the day.

She looks around his classroom, which is full of old maps, and pictures of all the old Civil War generals, and artifacts, and flags. It smells like dust, if dust has a smell. Her father's parents died before she was born, and her mother's parents live in San Diego, in a condo overlooking the Pacific, but this seems like a grandfatherly atmosphere. Justin would love this room, she thinks. She hopes Mr. Wakish will stick around long enough to have him in class.

Then she thinks, What if I have a baby? How old will it be by then?

"I'm just scared about something," she says. Unexpectedly, her eyes fill up with tears.

"Why should you be scared?" His voice is gentle. So gentle it catches her off guard.

"I think I'm pregnant!" she blurts out. Then she blushes, wishing she could take it back, explain, erase, rewind.

Mr. Wakish is shaking his head slowly. "Oh, dear," he says. "Dear, dear."

She's afraid she has shocked him. He's too old to be thinking about teenage pregnancies. She says quickly, "But don't worry, because I really know I'm not."

"How can you know that, my dear?" Mr. Wakish keeps shaking his head slowly, from side to side.

"I'm sure," she says. The panic is starting to come back, and that voice in her head, which had been startled into silence, starts up again, *You can't be absolutely sure.*

"Tell me about it," he says. He takes her hand.

She is hoping he can read her palm and reassure her, *No, of course not, you are absolutely not pregnant. You will go on a long journey. You will meet a dark, handsome stranger.* He just holds it in his thin, old, shaking hand. He is out of his depth, that's clear.

"Have you ever been with a boy?" he asks.

She nods, embarrassed—but also relieved to be talking about it to someone, anyone.

He hesitates. "With your clothes off?"

She nods again.

"And you touched him?" His voice is tremulous.

She is praying there isn't anything creepy about all these questions. She nods, and he sighs, deeply, and it is impossible

64

to tell if he is remembering something—his wife has been dead for years, she knows—or if he is sighing out of sorrow, or pleasure, or what. "But that's all?" She barely moves her head, but it is a nod. "And that's why you're afraid?"

He pats her hand twice and lets it go. "I don't think you're pregnant," he says. "From what you're telling me—I wouldn't know, of course, but I don't suppose so. But don't you think you ought to talk to your parents about this, Stephanie?"

"You're not going to call them, are you?" She isn't so much alarmed as mortified, at the idea.

"Oh, heavens no!" he says. "Certainly not. I just thought you might want to talk to them—about why you're so afraid."

"I will," she says. It seems like the fastest way to stop this conversation and she's suddenly completely embarrassed. "That's a great idea. I definitely will. Thank you, Mr. Wakish. I'm sorry about not paying attention in class. I really like history." Now she sounds like an idiot—or like she just wants a good grade. Actually, she would be happy if he would just flunk her and let it go at that.

He sighs again, another long deep sigh, and shuts his eyes. "Youth is always wasted on the young," he says. "Try not to worry so much—not to take foolish chances, of course. The whole world is a very narrow bridge, but the most important thing is not to be afraid at all."

"Which general said that?" she asks.

"A rabbi, back in the eighteenth century. Rabbi Nachman of Bratz. There's more than one way to be brave, my dear."

What Her Parents Think about Sex, Part One

It's not anything their family has ever discussed.

She asks her father, while Justin is upstairs taking a bath, and her father is alone, reading a science journal. "What do you think about sex?"

She didn't mean to startle him. He lets the magazine fall into his lap. "Sex?" he asks.

"Never mind," she says.

"You mean—premarital sex? Or sex in general?"

"Skip it," she says. "Really."

"Okay." He seems relieved to go back to his magazine. But after a few minutes, just when she thinks he's forgotten about it, he says, from behind the magazine covers, "Maybe you want to talk to your mother." It's part question, part answer, part apology.

"Good idea," she says.

What Her Parents Think about Sex, Part Two

"Mom, wake up," she says.

Clarissa opens her eyes. "Is it time to get up already?" she says. It is nine o'clock at night. Clarissa goes to bed early now, right after dinner, like a child. Justin stays up later than she does, watching old sit coms and laughing till he cries. Wiping his eyes. He's a strange child, old before his time. He likes the old comedies—classics, he calls them. His idol is Charlie Chaplin. He has a picture of the little hobo on his bedroom door.

"Do you think there's anything wrong with sex?" Stephanie asks.

"Wrong?" she says, "What do you mean, wrong?" Her mother struggles to sit up, to come awake.

"I mean, do you think it's bad?"

She's slow to answer. "Well," she says. "Bad." She struggles to wake up. Some instinct is telling her to open her eyes, to answer. "I wouldn't say bad. Dangerous, maybe ... powerful. Especially for someone your age."

"Look," the girl blurts out. "If you don't tell me it's okay to have sex sometime with someone you love, I'm going to end up as a crazy person. I'm going to wind up in a straitjacket."

"Are you asking my permission?" the mother asks. She seems startled, to say the least.

"No," the girl says. "I don't know, maybe. No, of course not. ... Yes."

"All right," Clarissa says. But it isn't clear what she's saying all right to. In a few minutes she's breathing evenly again. Sometimes the girl feels like the only one awake in a sleeping kingdom.

The Next Day

But the next day Clarissa has made an appointment for her daughter with Dr. Ray, the gynecologist.

"What for?" the daughter asks.

"So we can get you on some birth control," her mother says matter-of-factly. Stephanie just prays it isn't too late to do her any good.

And Sometimes

She thrills in her little power over him, though she doesn't understand the power; it's like having a magic wand that moves of its own volition. And his body is so ridiculously out in the open, so almost coarse compared to her own. The rough, dark bluish-black stubble of his beard when he doesn't shave for days. The springy hair on his legs, his bony knees, his long, long feet like the coffins of kings. And that strange knob of flesh that seems to be the secret center of him, which rises and falls and rises, and she can't begin to understand it all.

Pied-à-Terre

Denny shows her his father's apartment in Boston. That's where his law office is, and sometimes he has to work late, so he has a place in the middle of the city. It's very posh—a fountain in the lobby, one doorman to open the door for you, and another to watch him open it.

"You mean he sleeps here?" she asks.

"Not often," Denny says. "Not more than once or twice a week."

"But your house is only forty minutes away by train." Her own father wakes up at four in the morning sometimes so he can drive to a conference in Baltimore or Philadelphia, and drives back when it's all over.

"His work is exhausting," Denny says, a little peevishly.

"I see," she answers, because suddenly, she does really see. The apartment feels as neutral as a hotel room. But a few things make it different from the Pistil house. A bar, for one thing. A soft-looking watercolor, just above the king-sized bed in the bedroom. A vase of fresh pink roses on the bureau by the bed.

She looks away from the roses as if they were pornography she'd found in Mr. Pistil's desk drawer.

"What do you think?" Denny says, leading her over to the bed, beside the pink roses. She is thinking, *What man buys roses just for himself, for an apartment he uses only after work?* And she knows the answer: *No man.*

While she and Denny are on the bed, she feels this sadness, rising up through the box springs, like spending Christmas with a kid who still believes in Santa when you know it's just another grown-up lie.

The Other Woman

"I want to know about you and Anna," she says one evening at Denny's house, as if asking for a bedtime story. But her heart is pounding.

"It just sort of happened. It was very spontaneous."

"What does she look like?"

"I have a picture," Denny says. "If you really want to see."

She sits upright, tucking her legs beneath her, and he begins looking through some photos in an album till he comes to the right page. He turns the book around, as if this young woman has suddenly turned to face her. "Anna," he says.

The girl's skin is tanned, and her hair is long and black and loose. She has several rings on her hands, and what looks like a bracelet on one tanned ankle. She is wearing a long flowered skirt, and is half smiling toward someone or something just out of the frame.

She's not exactly pretty—her nose is hooked and her features are sharp; she looks a little like the Wicked Witch of the West in the movie *The Wizard of Oz,* but there's something about the way she stands, the way she smiles. She looks relaxed. She looks sexy.

Man on the Train

She and Denny take the train to Boston to look at the Young Picasso Retrospective at the Fine Arts Museum. She's never really loved Picasso, and Denny says she's got him all wrong.

Well, that must be so. When Picasso was twelve, he was painting better than most great artists, and not long after that, Picasso's own artist-father gave up painting, completely, forever. Stephanie thinks she understands how he felt.

Now, standing in the Fine Arts Museum, Stephanie loves the Blue Period best—"You would," Denny says kiddingly— a mother and child in a poverty ward, looking like Madonna and Child. Gaunt streetwalkers. Models with sad faces and voluptuous bodies. Afterward, they walk up Milk Street arm in arm. It's raining. She's having mild cramps, which makes her feel hopeful that her period is really in fact about to arrive. Denny holds an umbrella over their heads, and hangs on to her arm to keep her close. He is wearing a long beige raincoat, like a grownup.

A man with eyes hidden under impossibly heavy eyebrows directs them six blocks to the Atheneum, where Denny's parents are members. Stephanie has never been inside the building. Denny explains it's partly a museum, partly a library, and altogether a very cool place.

At the Atheneum he shows her the statue of a marble girl he says reminds him of her. He rests his hand on her naked foot, and it sends a pleasant shiver through

Stephanie. It is so quiet in there, it's as if they've all been turned into stone.

A skinny college boy is sleeping on a padded bench upstairs, with a book open on his chest: *How to Make the Best Use of Your Time.* He snores lightly. She and Denny leave so their laughter won't wake him.

On the train ride home Stephanie rests her head in Denny's lap. This is the most peaceful she's felt in his presence. They are in one of those four-seat squares, where passengers sit facing each other. They are riding the train backward. Raindrops fling themselves suicidally against the windows of the train and are spun off as the train moves faster. Stephanie shuts her eyes and strokes Denny's leg, long and muscular under the tan raincoat.

She keeps petting his leg till abruptly his hand seizes her wrist, stopping her. She looks up. A middle-aged stranger, sitting across from her, is holding her hand, shaking his head slightly and smiling. She realizes with horror that it's his leg she's been stroking all along, not Denny's. She sits bolt upright, blushing furiously.

Denny is asleep, slumped against the side of the train, mouth open. The man smiles at her reassuringly. His face is thin and drawn, he has thin straight blond hair and a blond mustache. She wishes she could sink through the seat and drop under the train, onto the rails. She wishes the earth would open up and swallow her whole. Her palm tingles with the remembered sensation of this other man's coat under her hand—heavier than Denny's trench coat, and silkier. A grownup's raincoat.

"I am so extremely sorry," she says, burning with shame. Why can't I keep my hands to myself! she thinks.

"That's all right," the man says. "Actually, it's the nicest thing that's happened to me all day."

Luckily there's no one else sitting next to him, watching. She sits with her spine poker-straight and keeps staring out the window till the man gets off at his stop. He wishes her a pleasant evening, and she says, "Good night," and "thank you for being so understanding," and at that point Denny wakes up, sleepily moving his long legs so the man can get out into the aisle, and asks, "What was that about?"

Mephisto

Mephisto doesn't write about damsels in distress, he creates them. People are afraid to put their poetry in the folders, to put in anything they actually care about. Suddenly there are lots of joke poems, limericks, and a few haiku as empty as vacant lots. No one is taking any chances.

Denny can't understand what she's so worked up about. "Just ignore him," he says. "We were once in track together. He's just a dumb jock."

"What did he do on the track team?" she asks. "He looks too big to be a good runner."

Denny shakes his head. "He isn't very fast," he agrees. "I dunno. I think he used to throw something. Throw something heavy."

"At people?" she asks.

Denny smiles and plays with her hair, mussing it up and pulling the curls over her eyes so she can't see. "Not as far as I know," he says.

In the Kingdom

In the kingdom of their high school, she is now royalty. It makes her realize how tiny that kingdom is, a locked box inside a closet, buried underground. The way a few boys follow after Denny, now a few pale girls begin trailing her. One girl even dyes her hair a lighter shade of red and begins dressing like her. If you blow on a mirror and the mirror fogs, that's the reflection. The same, only grayer.

Popularity isn't all it's cracked up to be.

"Oh, poor you," Lisa says. Their friendship is harsh angles these days, with Lisa resentful and Stephanie apologetic, and everything that was easy between them shut out or shut in or shut up. What she feels is, trapped in a snare of her own making.

Relief

At last it comes, when she isn't looking, not expecting it, for once. The bowl is bright red, decorated with one sheet of white paper, like a piece of gift-wrap paper, also stained red. She has never been so happy in her life to put on a sanitary napkin.

Dining at Home

The first time Denny finally comes to the house for supper, her father talks only about suspension bridges, and her mother makes Girl Scout Stew. Girl Scout Stew is a favorite of Justin's and used to be one of Stephanie's, too. It's perfect for a little kid's taste buds—ground beef and vegetable soup, with some canned mushrooms, or little potatos or pearl onions or corn, if you want to get fancy about it. They add everything they can think of, but nothing seems to rescue the meal.

Denny says it's delicious, but doesn't mean it. He doesn't work very hard at pretending he does. Justin eats like a pig.

At Denny's house they serve things like Chicken Cordon Bleu and Trout Almondine. She's even seen Denny help his mom make Chicken Kiev—rolling the pounded, boneless, skinless breasts around the herbed butter and deftly tucking it all under.

She's pretty sure she could make Girl Scout Stew—it was something her mother taught the troop when she was in Junior Girl Scouts, earning badges. Each of the mothers had to teach a skill. No one invited the fathers to do anything. Her father would have liked teaching the kids about science and astronomy. She thought they'd ask Clarissa to teach sculpture, which would have been fun, even in a show-offy way, but instead they asked her to teach cooking, so she shrugged and invented Girl Scout Stew, and they've been eating it once or twice a month ever since.

Her father and Justin talk about their favorite bridges. Justin's is the Verrazano, in New Jersey. The father favors the Bourne Bridge. Denny looks bored and uncomfortable. He mumbles something about stone bridges in England.

Denny asks Clarissa about her work, but she keeps leaving the table on some excuse, going for dinner rolls, or an extra napkin, or more juice, saying, "Oh, never you mind about me." She seems determined not to know him, and keeps looking at Stephanie and Denny distrustfully, as if they might disappear under the table any minute.

Kit, Again

Diane and Kit and Denny and Stephanie go for a picnic on the bay side of Cape Cod. A December day. They take their bicycles, which Denny loads into his mother's black van.

Somehow, the two young women find themselves sitting together in the backseat while Kit and Denny are up front. Diane raises her eyebrows. "Gee, just like the Flintstones," Stephanie says. The boys can't hear them because they've got the jazz radio station on full blast and have to yell even to hear one another.

When they finally get there, Kit drags Diane away again, right away, and Denny and Stephanie sit in the car with the heater on because it turns out it's much too cold in the park. At least it is for her.

She wants to tell him about what's been happening to her all month, about her fear of being pregnant, but every time she opens her mouth it's as if a great cold wind blows directly down her throat into her heart. She huddles near the heater to stay warm.

When Kit and Diane get back, clothes rumpled, pieces of brown grass sticking to their clothing and hair, Kit barely looks at anyone and, hardly moving his lips, says, "Let's go for a ride." He and Denny and Diane dutifully get on their bikes and circle the park for twenty minutes or so.

Stephanie stays inside, smoking cigarette after cigarette—a bad habit she's picked up from Denny and his chain-smoking father—with the window rolled down just enough to let the smoke out, and the heater on full blast. For no reason she can think of, she gets very depressed, and when she's not holding a cigarette she just holds her hands in her lap, trembling, and when she sees the three figures coming closer her heart sinks, and when they circle away again, it rises just a little, and then sinks again, on and on like that for what seems like forever.

Proposal

The Pistils invite Stephanie to spend part of the weekend in Boston at their apartment. Her job is to make sure her parents approve.

Her father, much to her embarrassment, insists on an official summit meeting among all the parents. So the Pistils come to the insane asylum for coffee and cake.

Mrs. Pistil looks around the living room as if they've buried a cat under the African artifacts and Moroccan pillows. Stephanie sees the house through her eyes: messy, too many bright colors, too many flowers and flowering plants cluttering up the place, too many earth tones, too much homemade sculpture, too much everything. Mr. Pistil has driven his Mercedes and is wearing a sixteen hundred dollar suit from Armani. It occurs to Stephanie, and not for the first time, that he is sexier than his son, even with the goofy toupee he wears when he's not doing a comb-over with the little hair that's left. Still, there is something kingly about him, whereas Denny seems like an imposter—grim Prince Hamlet wandering around the court looking for trouble and a crown.

Clarissa shows up in her ceramics apron, wiping clayey hands on her jeans.

"Nice to meet you," she says. "Can't shake hands," waving one of them in the air to demonstrate.

Stephanie and Denny send desperate messages with just their eyes. They are sent into the kitchen on some excuse. Denny sticks his head in the refrigerator and keeps it there, as if hoping to preserve himself. She positions herself at the crack in the door. There appear to be intermittent murmurs of uncomfortable polite conversation about the upcoming weekend—museum visit, possible theater tickets.

Then Stephanie's father's voice, loud and clear. "I just want to know one thing," he says. "Does your son love my daughter?"

She peeks through the crack in the door. There is a shocked silence, as if her father had made a loud, rude noise. Mrs. Pistil doesn't know where to look. Clarissa is standing as still as one of her own sculptures, but she is watching every move. Mr. Pistil shifts uncomfortably in his chair, crossing and recrossing his legs, and breaks the long silence to say, "Well, I think he does. It seems to me that he does. Yes."

"That's the only thing that matters to me," her father says stubbornly. "I'm not talking about marriage or anything like that. They're both far too young to be contemplating anything like that. I just want to know if he loves her."

Mrs. Pistil cranes her head to get a better look at this bizarre creature. Mr. Pistil looks annoyed. One senses he's about to glance at his watch. He does, and frowns. "I suppose you'd have to ask Denny," he says. "Do you want me to call him in here?"

"That won't be necessary," her father answers. "I'll take your word for it."

"Okay, then," her mom says. "More cake, anyone?"

For some reason, no one wants more cake.

Her parents walk the Pistils out to the car. Clarissa comes back inside first, but her dad stays out there a little while, admiring Mr. Pistil's car. They all lean over to study the tires. Maybe they're checking to make sure they won't explode. Then they inspect the front grill. Everyone shakes hands with the father of the bride-never-to-be.

Then he comes inside, looking so tired, his hair so rumpled, she can't bring herself to say a harsh word. Wasn't he trying to protect her? Secretly she thinks he is sweet, if pathetic. He's got a science magazine and is pretending to read, but it's just lying there in his lap, and his squarish hand is resting on top of it, just enough to keep it from sliding away.

"That family," he says, "makes me feel like a poor Welshman."

And despite herself, Stephanie knows how he feels.

Denny and His Father

"My father's staying home more these days," Denny tells her. He sounds pleased. "He hasn't used his apartment in almost a month. And he's on his new medication. If he drinks while he's taking it, he'll get very, very ill."

"Could he die?" she asks.

"I don't know," Denny says. "Maybe. But I don't think he'll try it. He promised my mother he won't."

"You really love your father, don't you."

"I admire him," Denny says. "More than anyone else in the world. But I'm not sure if that's the same thing."

If someone asked Stephanie, she'd have to say she loved her father more than any man in the world, but she's not sure she admires him.

Maybe, she thinks, the problem is that she is admiring the wrong things.

Not Poetry

Someone has written on one of her poems, in a familiar handwriting: *You call this poetry?*

Ben is sitting alone at a library table, reading. She marches over to him and slams the poem down in front of his startled face. "Yes, I call it poetry," she says.

He looks up, his round blue eyes growing rounder. Then he says, "I didn't write this. I didn't even read this poem." He picks it up and looks at it a moment. "Seems like poetry to me," he says.

She's full of a manic energy now that she doesn't know what to do with. It's as if she can't find a way to shut off this machine, her rage, her voice. "Well, you've written terrible things on other people's poems," she says, snatching the piece of paper out of his hands.

"I tell the truth," he says, still in a mild voice. "Why don't you sit down? Would you like to sit down and talk?"

And amazingly enough, she sits.

More about Ben

Tacitly, they meet during eighth period, the last period of the day. He has study hall, she has free reading. They talk through the last bell, through the late bell, through the last athletic bus leaving for home.

"I've missed wrestling practice," he says.

"Is that bad?" she asks him.

He shrugs. "Coach won't like it."

"Will they throw you off the team?"

A certain light in his eyes, amusement. "I don't think so."

"Are you that good?" she asks, daring him to brag.

"I'm a better wrestler than I am a poet," he says. "So, you think I should stop writing on people's papers?"

"I do," she says.

"Then I will."

"That would be good." She knows that her lips are chapped— this always happens in the winter—so badly chapped that they are actually cracked and bleeding. She tries to cover her mouth with one hand.

"I can't hear you," he says. "Can you take your hand away from your mouth?"

She does.

"Beautiful," he says.

Problem and Solution

Problem: three theater tickets, five theatergoers. Denny is dying to go; therefore, so is his younger sister Rhea. There is no question of Mrs. Pistil not going—she's the one who got the tickets in the first place. Denny wants Stephanie to come. Mrs. Pistil wants Mr. Pistil to come. No one but Rhea wants Rhea to come. That is the story of her life.

Solution: They'll all eat dinner at a fancy restaurant in Boston, then three of them will go to the theater, and later that night everyone will stay in the apartment—Mr. and Mrs. Pistil in the bedroom, Rhea, Denny and Stephanie in sleeping bags and on the couch, in the living room. Rhea claims the couch immediately.

All of this is okay because Mr. Pistil told her dad that his son, Denny, probably loves her. Denny certainly says he does often enough. He says it all the time. He says it mournfully, as if he's just heard bad news.

And he writes it. Sometimes he writes her two or three letters a day, especially over the weekends. His handwriting is black and scrawly, and she can't actually read all of the words, but there are so many of them, pouring out all over the page, that it doesn't seem to matter if she misses a few. The letters are desperate, full of reassurances, and yet they make her more and more uneasy. Something is wrong. She thinks of that line from Shakespeare, "Methinks he doth protest too much."

Mr. Pistil is the first one who says he doesn't care about going to the play, in fact he hates most theater. Mrs. Pistil looks so disappointed and angry that Stephanie immediately jumps in to agree. Now everyone looks shocked, but Denny, Rhea, and Mrs. Pistil look a little pleased, too, because their dilemma is solved.

Mr. Pistil and Stephanie will take a taxi back to the apartment after dinner and—and—play Scrabble? sit at separate tables playing solitaire? get drunk? hopefully not, since Mr. Pistil is on medicine that makes you almost die if you try drinking while you're taking it. Maybe they'll just watch TV. Stephanie is not actually worried about it. The truth is, she feels more comfortable with Mr. Pistil than with his son.

Dinner is at a posh continental restaurant with pale pink tablecloths and napkins. She and Rhea go investigate the ladies' room, which is disappointingly plain. Not even those perfume dispensers. Just a basket with towels in the same pale pink as the table linens.

The restaurant serves things like rabbit and snails—only in French, of course, which Denny has to translate since Stephanie is taking Spanish. She barely touches her food because the place makes her nervous and the waiters all seem to be waiting for someone to drop or spill something; they stand around together watching the guests, but she artfully rearranges things on her plate, and Mr. Pistil is the only one who seems to notice. She often thinks she is with the wrong Pistil male.

"At least eat the salad," he tells her quietly, when no one else is looking. "This isn't healthy. Eat something. Anything. You've got to keep your blood sugar up."

In the Taxi

It feels strange, like the two of them are on a date. She wonders if she should call her father and make Mr. Pistil tell him that he loves her, too. She deliberately tucks herself away in the back left-hand corner of the cab, so their legs won't accidentally touch. The hard part, the embarrassing part, is that she wants them to touch, and then she immediately tells herself, *That is so twisted. You are so weird.*

Pied-à-Terre Revisited

Mr. Pistil excuses himself and makes a phone call from his bedroom—the one where the roses were. She can hear the low murmur of his voice, and at first everything seems to be going fine, because he laughs a few times, sweetly, in a happy voice she's never heard before. Then she hears him say, "Please don't," and "Don't say that, for god's sake," and then he stops talking.

Stephanie hears something that might be a sob, though she hopes it is a cough. The water runs in the bathroom faucet, and after a while he comes out with his face and his hair wet, so it's impossible to tell if he's been washing his face or crying, or both.

She has to pretend not to understand any of this.

He turns on the TV, which is enormous, the largest, flattest thing she's ever seen—it hangs on the wall like a huge painting. They both watch some stupid comedy show for a while, and then he turns his head to her and asks, "Do you like this?" and she says not particularly, and he clicks it off. She tells him please not to turn it off for her sake. "No," he says. "Maybe I'll read for a while."

"Good idea," she says, to be encouraging. Then, so it'll look like she has something important to do, and as if she can keep herself entertained, she says, "I think I'll do some homework," even though she doesn't have any.

"Good idea," he says. He takes a book off a shelf and walks back into the bedroom. Fifteen or twenty minutes go by. Then he comes out into the living room and asks if she wants a brandy.

"No thanks," she says. She's not actually old enough to drink yet. Doesn't Mr. Pistil know that? Maybe he knows but just doesn't care.

He pours himself a drink from the bar, and she watches him without thinking much of anything till she remembers about the medicine he's taking, which she's probably not supposed to know about, but she blurts out, anyway, "Hey! Is that a good idea?"

He turns from the bar to look at her. "Is what a good idea?"

"That," she says, not quite looking at the bar but more or less toward it. "You know, that." She is afraid to offend him, but even more afraid to watch him die.

"This?" He lifts the glass of brandy and quickly drains it. "Oh yes. I think it's a great idea."

She waits for him to start foaming at the mouth, or fall down writhing, like Madame Bovary in the novel, but nothing happens, except he says, "You sure you don't want a drink? I can get you a soda, if you'd like."

"No, that's all right," she says. Her eyes are fixed to his every movement. It's like watching a horror movie. She has to say something, do something. "Aren't you taking that medicine?" she finally asks. She winces a little, waiting for him to storm at her. There is always something a little terrifying about Mr. Pistil—and unpredictable. Like a thundercloud. You never know what form he's going to take.

"What medicine?" His voice is faraway and disinterested, as if he's not even listening. Denny must have been mistaken. Mr. Pistil is not a stupid man. And he looks perfectly normal. He pours himself another drink and sits on the sofa. "You like this place?" he asks. "My wife, decorated. It." He says it very slowly, like that. Almost contemptuously.

"It's very nice," she says. "Boston's a wonderful city."

"You only think that because you're young," he says. He starts in on the second drink. "Boston is a city for the young. I don't think I was ever that young." He looks at Stephanie over his drink. "You're not all that young, yourself."

"I'm seventeen," she says.

"That's not what I mean." He finishes the drink and closes his eyes. "I'm tired."

Then he sort of slumps over sideways in his chair, and before he can actually hit the ground, she leaps out of her seat and catches him. A perfect catch. It is the most athletic thing she's ever done in her life, and no one is even there to see it. Now he is deadweight in her arms.

His skin is beaded with sweat. He opens his eyes. His eyes are dark brown, totally unlike his son's. There's no light shining back at her from those eyes. "Feel sick," he says.

It is so strange, holding this strange man in her arms, and she's also afraid that she might drop him, because he's surprisingly heavy. He's built compactly. A mustache and beard nearly hide his mouth. His nose is beaky. She's never had time to notice all these things before.

She takes a pillow from the sofa and places it under his head.

"I'm going to call nine-one-one," she tells him. "Then I'll be right back."

"No need—" he says thickly, but she runs into the bedroom, which is now without roses. The lady on the phone says she'll send someone right away, but Stephanie doesn't know if that means two minutes or two hours. What if he dies there? In her arms?

She runs back into the living room and crouches next to the glass coffee table. At least he is still breathing. She says, "Mr. Pistil." He opens his eyes, barely. "Stay awake, okay?" she says.

She's heard that if people have traumatic injuries—like concussions, or if they break their necks—you're supposed to try to keep them awake and alert. She doesn't know anything about this medicine, but his skin is pale greenish white. Her mother would know how to sculpt this.

He groans.

Stephanie lifts his head up and puts it in her lap, and doesn't bother him anymore. She prays that he's just asleep, that he's not dying, not already dead. She wishes she knew how to take a pulse, but when she holds his wrist it still feels like a live thing.

There's a glass display case in the living room just in front of her. Its shelves are filled with what looks like imported crystal—wine glasses and champagne glasses and crystal goblets, and a vase that looks like a wavy glass curve, and one or two elegant paperweights, and a cut-glass bowl that sends rainbows all over the room if she turns her head a certain way.

She doesn't dare move any other part of her body. She doesn't want to jar him.

"Are you all right?" she whispers, bending her head close. His beard is prickly against her skin. Her father is smooth-shaven, nothing like Mr. Pistil. He doesn't answer, his eyes are closed, but he is definitely still breathing. She finds ways of moving her head without moving the rest of her body, keeping her eyes on the bright crystal in the lighted case. The rest of the room is dark, and she almost strokes Mr. Pistil's head, but then she doesn't want to touch his hair, because what if the toupee comes off in her hand? She can't bear the idea of someone dying untouched, either, which seems even worse than holding a loose toupee, so she compromises by patting his shoulder, stroking the soft material of his jacket, which reminds her of the middle-aged man on the train.

"Everything is going to be all right," she tells him, "someone is on the way," and after a while, feeling desperate, she recites the only two poems she knows by heart, "Stopping by Woods on a Snowy Evening" by Robert Frost, and "The Song of Wandering Aengus" by W. B. Yeats. She says them over and over. If he gets sick of them, he doesn't complain.

Mr. Pistil really does look deathly ill. If that's what this medicine is supposed to do, then it's working like a charm. Once he murmurs a woman's name. Another time he says something that sounds like "Alabama." Sometimes he licks his lips, but she's afraid to give him anything to eat or drink, even water. She read somewhere that if someone ingests poison, you're supposed to give them a piece of bread to absorb the poison, but she's afraid to leave him. She has a superstition that if she leaves him alone for even a split second, he'll die, and if she tries to feed him anything, he'll choke.

So she just sits, his head growing heavier every second, and her legs falling asleep; the only lights coming from the distant city, lit up for the holidays; the display case filled with expensive sparking crystal, and darkness all around them.

Company

Denny, his sister, and his mother walk straight into this five minutes before the ambulance arrives.

"Oh no," says Mrs. Pistil faintly.

Denny stops in his tracks, straight and still. The look he turns on Stephanie is cold, dark and full of judgment; it turns her blood to ice. Her mouth opens and closes, silent. His sister Rhea begins to scream.

Stephanie struggles to stand up, but it's impossible, as if Mr. Pistil has grown rooted into her body and now the two of them are cemented to the carpeted floor of the apartment. She can't stop babbling. "He took a drink, I called nine-one-one. I'm so sorry. Is he going to be okay?" she says from the floor, and Mrs. Pistil says, in a very sharp voice, "Of course he is," and then, "You did exactly the right thing, Stephanie, thank you," and, "No one can stop him; don't blame yourself," but Denny refuses to look at her and then the doorbell rings and everything happens very quickly all at once, and her lap feels suddenly naked when they take Mr. Pistil's head away and pick him up as if he weighs nothing at all and load him onto a stretcher.

Denny steps away, his face a mask. He looks not worried but disapproving as the emergency workers lift his father higher.

When one arm falls away from Mr. Pistil's body, someone just moves the arm and drops it back over his chest, as if he's not a person anymore.

The Long Drive Home

Sometime during the night the hospital calls to say that Mr. Pistil is doing fine, and everyone goes home at three in the morning, with Denny driving all the way and murmuring quietly to his mother, while Rhea lies stretched out in the middle seat of the van crying, and finally falls asleep. Stephanie sits alone at the back of the van alongside the beachballs and kites and empty water bottles. Invisible. Denny never kisses her at all, that night. The coldness in his face never thaws. He is far away. She feels blamed, though no one says so out loud.

She's given the second bed in Rhea's room, where she sleeps, or tries to sleep. Denny says good night to her at the door without touching or looking at her. His voice is brittle. Rhea cries herself to sleep.

The room is large and cool, the walls are painted red. Sometime before dawn breaks, Stephanie gets up and walks all the way home through the murky grayish-blue vapor of four a.m. because she doesn't want to be there when everyone wakes up and has to face whatever happens next.

The First Time

It is the first time they have been out anywhere, alone together, since the night Mr. Pistil drank and got sick. They haven't talked about it, but Denny has been acting wooden around her and seems to be avoiding her in the halls. Finally one day at lunch he says stiffly, barely moving his lips, "I hope you won't feel you have to share what happened with anyone."

"Of course not," she says. "Who would I tell?"

"Your little friend Lisa," he says. "Or that character Ben."

"I wouldn't tell anyone," she says. "I didn't even tell my parents. I said your dad got a headache and that's why we came home early."

"Oh," he says, thawing visibly. "Well. Okay, then. Thanks."

That Character Ben

She and Ben sometimes stay after school talking in the library. They don't arrange it, but it seems whenever she's there, he shows up within five minutes, ten minutes at most. They sit in the same two upholstered chairs near the fiction section.

She could not begin to say what they talk about. Unexpectedly, he is funny. He makes her laugh so hard that she ends up on the library floor, laughing till there are tears in her eyes—stories about his father, who is a big, tough guy; apparently, even bigger and tougher than Ben. He draws her cartoons of the literary-magazine meetings. He makes himself out to be the biggest jerk in the world. He watches her laughing; he clowns to make her laugh harder. He has absolutely no shame.

Denny has been busy, on the other hand, with the yearbook. He wants her to join the staff, but the whole idea of a yearbook is strange to her. She just doesn't get it. It's not as if they're all having such a great time in high school that they'd never want to forget a single second.

"It's not about that," Denny says, frowning. "Besides, it would look good on your resume."

"I don't have a resume," Stephanie says. "I'm only seventeen years old."

"On your college applications, then. You do plan to go to college, don't you?"

They have gotten nastier with each other, like two dogs caught snarling in the same dark, cramped cage.

But now it is a Saturday morning, and they are just sitting in his house calmly listening to music.

Mr. Pistil is whistling downstairs—he has a very piercing, not very melodic but jaunty whistle. He knocks on Denny's door and is holding a box in his hands, a small black jewelry box.

He holds it out to Stephanie and says, "For you. A little thank you present."

She says, "You didn't have to."

He smiles wryly and says, "That's why I wanted to. Open it."

Denny has stiffened next to her, so she knows this wasn't anything planned in advance; this is a surprise to him, too.

Inside the jewelry box lies a big silver ring with three coral stones set vertically, a long row. When she puts it on, it almost covers her whole finger. She feels herself blushing—the curse of red hair! She murmurs into the box, "Thank you."

"You like it?" Mr. Pistil says, amused.

"I love it," she tells the inside of the box.

It feels like it belongs to her, it is for her. Denny picks up her hand and looks at the ring. "It's big on you," he says.

After Mr. Pistil has left the room, Denny kisses her roughly and says, "When?"

She knows what he means. "Soon," she says.

"How soon?"

"I don't know," she says. Her hand feels heavy, as if it doesn't belong to her, weighed down with the new ring. She puts it on his knee and looks at her fingers, which look grown-up and long. "Tonight? Is that soon enough?" But even as he laces his fingers through hers and smiles into her eyes, she wonders if she's said that just to get it over with.

It Doesn't

It doesn't hurt. Not as much as she had thought. Somewhere along the line, she had confused stories she heard about labor with stories she'd heard about the first time, and thought they'd be about the same. It doesn't mean as much, either. Now that she's on birth control, she isn't worried about getting pregnant. She's more worried about becoming empty than full.

There's a sharp, shooting pain, and afterward, her legs feel weak and shaky and yes, there is blood on the beach towel Denny has spread underneath them.

"Look at that," she says.

The next day he sends a gift to her house—a bouquet of six balloons and six lollipops. It seems like a strange way to enter into womanhood, in the guise of a child.

Afterward

The second, third, and fourth times, he comes so quickly he has barely gotten inside her before it's over, and he seems out of breath, winded, like a runner.

Where is he rushing to?

Then he holds very still and doesn't move. He stares up at the ceiling, like an ancient Pharaoh. His body seems stiff and cold.

He apologizes.

He is suffering from something he calls "disassociation." He feels like he's out of his own body, out of his room, out of town. He says it's nothing she's doing. Once, he punches the wall in his bedroom and leaves a fist-shaped hole in the plaster above her head. They both stare at it, as if it had just appeared, bloomed there mysteriously. He proclaims his everlasting love for her. Why is this so difficult? Is it like this for everyone? He weeps. He asks her to hold him. She does.

She cannot find the clue to unfreeze him.

One Day

One day she finds her mother asleep at three-thirty in the afternoon, sleeping so deeply that for a second or two, standing in the doorway to the bedroom, Stephanie believes she is dead. Her mother's hair is fanned out like a golden crown around her head. The flowered coverlet neither rises nor falls. There is an almost empty bottle of pills on the little bedside table.

She steps close to the bed. "Mom?" Maybe the bottle of pills was almost empty that morning? "Mom?"

She is so tired of being the only grownup in the house. So tired, for an instant she considers climbing in beside her mother and going into her own deep sleep.

She raises her voice a little. "Mom? Mom!"

Still no answer. She rushes to her mother's bureau, looking for something, anything useful, thinking what to do. She snatches up an ornate silver hand mirror and holds it under her mother's nose. The surface of the mirror instantly clouds over.

Stephanie sobs with relief. She calls Dr. Davin, her mother's psychiatrist, and the next thing she knows, they both have appointments to see him.

It feels as if something is starting to lift, just a little. Or maybe it's getting a little worse, maybe she is actually falling deeper into a cold, dark something. But either way, she is in motion, and anything seems better than holding still.

Quitting

Ben quit the literary magazine, Lisa tells her furiously, as if it's all her fault. She and Lisa haven't been getting along too well lately. Maybe she's lost the knack of getting along.

"Why are you blaming me?" Stephanie asks.

"As if you didn't know," Lisa says.

"I don't." They are throwing a handball against the brick wall behind the cafeteria. How many years have they been friends? Six, seven, eight, nine. Stephanie catches the ball and forces Lisa to look at her. "Stop a minute," she says.

Lisa is out of breath, clutching her ribs. She goes and sits on a bench. Stephanie sits beside her.

"Listen," she says. "If you like Ben—I mean if you like him that way—just tell me, and I'll stop."

"I don't!" Lisa's dark eyes flash darker. "Not at all."

"Are you sure? Really?"

Lisa laughs, a sharp barking laugh. "One thousand per-cent sure."

"Honest?"

"For Pete's sake, Stephanie!"

Suddenly Stephanie feels light and energetic. She runs up to the brick wall and pushes her feet hard against it, springing off. Flying through the air. Giddy.

New Medicine

Her mother is on a brand new medicine. Experimental. It gives her headaches, dry mouth, indigestion, and nausea. She is losing hair in clumps, on the pillow, in the shower. Golden strands of it everywhere. She falls asleep at the dinner table, then wakes in the middle of the night. Food tastes funny to her. Everything smells funny—the gas station, the hallway, the food she is cooking, the food she throws away still in its plastic wrap.

But she says she is feeling better; almost normal. She is up to her elbows in clay, working, even selling some of her pieces to a gallery in Boston.

Four bright pink pills a day.

Fair Diane

One mild day just before Christmas break, Stephanie takes a walk around the school during lunch period. What she would really like to do is to go find Ben, but she has been avoiding him. Denny seems relieved. He would never stoop to telling her he's jealous. Not of anyone. Even so. She tells herself, Ben's just acting nice but he's still a bully.

Probably he makes fun of me behind my back. She doesn't believe it. Still, the feeling of disloyalty persists.

So she goes for a walk. It's like a walk around a prison yard—people sneaking cigarettes out back, the stubbled bare look of the fences and fields. Mrs. Serbuck, the assistant principal, paces the perimeter, and is out now doing just that. But when Stephanie waves, she doesn't snarl or order her back inside the school, just waves back.

The winter thaw has left puddles all over the athletic field. Diane is sitting up against the brick wall behind the cafeteria, practically curled into a ball.

Her head is down, tucked between her knees. She is a moody girl. Stephanie assumes she's been crying. They haven't seen much of each other lately, and never outside of school since their last visit to Kit's.

"Diane?" she says. But when Diane looks up, her eyes are clear. She looks like one of those fifteenth-century portraits of a young madonna, or an Italian nobleman's daughter.

"Kit and I broke up," she says, as if she were saying hi.

gold skinny wedding bands. It is hard to know what to say. Luckily, Mr. Pistil isn't there to see the look of dread on his son's face. She can only imagine the expression on her own.

Here is the best Christmas gift she gives him. She takes the boxes out of his big hands and says, "I'll put them away somewhere for now. Tell your father we said thank you."

Neither of them even tries on the rings.

At School

Ben finds her in the library during lunch. She's been going home straight after school. She is afraid to look at Ben, at his full lips, his muscled body, his anxious smile. He is too full of life.

He doesn't seem angry, the way she thought he would be. Instead he says, "Are you all right? Is there somebody I need to hurt?"

She laughs for the first time in a week, which makes her cracked lips bleed, which makes her cover her mouth with her hand again.

"Oh, no." Stephanie crouches beside her. "I'm so sorry. Why did he break up with you?"

Diane half smiles. "Actually, I broke up with him," she says.

"You did?" Stephanie is embarrassed. "But why? You were crazy about him, weren't you?"

"Maybe that's why," Diane says. She toys with the bottom of her blue jeans, poking at a loose thread on the pants cuff. "He wasn't crazy about me." She stares off, across the field, which is pure dead brown grass now, despite the thaw; not a sign of green anywhere. "He never kissed when we—you know—when we were fooling around. Not once."

"Maybe he's—maybe he's shy," Stephanie says. She pictures his harsh sharp face.

"No, he's not shy," Diane says. She hesitates. "Scared, not shy."

She stands and dusts off the back of her jeans with both hands. Her large, penetrating, shining blue eyes lock on to Stephanie's for an instant. "Ask Denny about it sometime," she says.

Then she changes the subject. She starts talking about the writers she likes: Virginia Woolf and Agatha Christie and P. G. Wodehouse and E. M. Forster, till Stephanie feels dizzy with the number of books she's never even heard of.

"You and I should get together," Diane says. "I do read poetry, you know. I mean, we should get together, just the two of us, not with Kit or Denny or Jeanette or anybody else." Her voice trails off, as if she's lost energy or confidence. She sounds like a child. "Do you want to do that sometime?"

"Yes, I do," Stephanie says. And she thinks, A new friend.

It would be good to have a friend.

Merry Christmas

Justin stands under the tree, moving right, then left, then darting right again, jumping on the balls of his quick feet. "There!—no, there! Higher, a little higher, Stephie."

And there she is, dressed in the same black slacks and turtleneck she's worn all week, her arm stretched high over her head to reach the topmost branch. It is the most exercise she's had in days. She fixes the star to the bran with a red twist tie, and says, "Is it all right?"

"It's perfect!" he calls.

She steps back, winded from this bit of exertion. "Okay, then." She collapses onto the red velvet sofa in the living room. The star looks crooked to her, but she'd rather die than admit it and have to start all over again.

Beneath the tree are presents: lumpy presents wrapped by Justin, and store-wrapped presents from their relatives who live far away, and presents from Denny, too many presents. They opened them together the night-before-the-night-before Christmas. Then Denny and his family are flying to Jamaica for the holidays, back after the New Year.

She gave him: a new pair of gloves, a cashmere scarf, tw CDs, a straw hat for Jamaica and the *Collected Poems Wallace Stevens*.

He gave her: beaded earrings, a necklace strung v African beads and garnets, a flowered T-shirt.

Mr. Pistil had a gift for each of them, too, in matchin; blue Tiffany boxes. They open the boxes; inside are

"Poor kid," he says.

Mephisto, the evil one. He takes a handkerchief out of his pocket and gives it to her.

The Letter

Denny is sitting on his bed holding the letter in wonderment. He shows it to her, and her heart sinks so hard so fast, like an elevator shooting down a shaft, she thinks she is going to pass out. It is a love letter, it must be from the girl with the tan skin and the silver bracelets, but no, there is something too fierce and hotly angry, too apologetic in this love letter. Something different; she can't put her finger on it.

She scans to the bottom and finds: *I love you desperately. Kit.*

Part of her wants to laugh, but something in Denny's face stops her. And it isn't really funny. She supposes Kit is desperate; this explains a lot.

The question comes out before she has a chance to think about it. "Are you in love with him?" she asks.

Still in wonderment, still bewildered. He holds the letter in his big hand. "I don't know," he says.

Somebody Lied

Someone lied to someone. Lisa is not speaking to her anymore. Her small thin dark face flames with anger. She is the new editor in chief. She and Ben had a falling out.

"Not over me," Stephanie says. "It wasn't about me, right?"

Lisa won't answer. She keeps walking down the hall—rapid, jerky steps.

"But you told me you didn't even like him!" Stephanie says.

Lisa swings on her, her body moving quick as a snake's. "Well, I lied! If you were any kind of friend, you would have known I was lying!"

"I detest you," she adds over her shoulder. Her face twists. "I doubt I ever even liked you."

Stephanie doubts it, too.

Descending

She tells Denny not to worry. He tells her not to be afraid. She tells him not to be afraid. He tells her not to worry.

"What difference does it make?" she says. "You're allowed to be however you are."

But this only irritates him further. "I don't know how I am," he says. "Quit pushing me."

"I wasn't pushing you."

"Please don't leave me."

She has read that outer space has a scent. It smells like ash. Which makes sense, when you think about it—all those meteors and stars and moons burned up. Their kisses used to feel like winter air; too light, too frightened. Now they taste like outer space.

Why is it so hard to live inside a body?

She finds herself standing in a pose she's seen so often in her mother—the pose of a hanged man. Standing limp, arms dangling, no strength to lift the hands or head.

What Makes Her Cry

The news. A dead mouse in the trap her father set in the attic last week. Lisa never returning any of her calls. Justin getting his first bad grade. The smell of onions frying. Denny's worried face; his long, scrawled letters. Long-distance telephone commercials.

Hearing about a bus crash makes her burst into tears in study hall. Finding someone else ate the last frozen fruit pop in the house, because juice bars are about the only thing she can still stomach. Overhearing her parents arguing. Christmas Muzak at all the shopping plazas and malls. Old people. Babies. Friendship cards. Burning her tongue on hot coffee.

Everything.

She Knows

Nothing fruitful could come of these strange unions with Denny. They are quite a pair. She is sick to her stomach; he is frozen. Their lovemaking is a wrestling match no one is winning. "I will not let thee go except thou bless me."

No one is willing to be first to let go. Not first. Not yet.

Not Home

Mother sleeps. Daughter sleeps. When the phone rings, she jerks awake violently, as if she is being called from a long, long way off. She must rise through layers of another world to reach the receiver. It seems like too much bother. Better to sleep. Sleep is vastly underrated.

Lisa never calls again. Diane calls. The school calls.

Her mother appears in a pink terry cloth robe at the doorway to her room. "Why are you still sleeping?" she says. Her voice rings. "I think—Stephanie, I think you're having a nervous breakdown!"

Does she sound frightened, or triumphant? Like mother, like daughter.

Stephanie turns over and goes back to sleep.

Shrinking

Dr. Davin, the psychiatrist, is just handsome enough to be distracting. He looks a little like the actor on TV who plays an emergency rescue worker, which doesn't help her feeling that he's there to rescue her and all she has to do is wait.

But she has to want to get better, he says. She has to work at it, talk about what's going on. Things move along very slowly, like one of those glaciers that shaped New England over the course of a few million years.

"What's happening down there?" is the first thing he asks.

"I'm not eating much," she tells him. The understatement of the universe.

"Why not?"

"I guess I'm just not hungry."

"I see," he says, but not as if he does see. "Still throwing up a lot?"

She says, "I can't seem to keep anything down." They have already done every kind of physical examination on earth. "I don't have any friends. Lisa hates me."

"What's going on with Denny?" he asks.

"He says he loves me. But we mostly just sit there and look at each other. I just can't swallow it anymore."

"Interesting expression," Dr. Davin says. "You think maybe it has something to do with your eating problems?"

Just rescue me.

It Isn't Better

It isn't better with Denny gone on vacation. It isn't worse. She seems to be below all of that, and everyone alive and everything that matters is above her. It is as if she's been locked in the cellar, and can still hear the rest of the world walking around. Her mother calls for her, pauses, calls again, roams from room to room.

I'm down here, she wants to call. But she is down too far to call.

Panic

She wakes one morning pinned like a butterfly to the bed with fear. Her heart is beating wildly and she's only just opened her eyes. The clock says it's 9 a.m. She can't lift her arms, they seem weighted down, and her forehead is sweaty, but she is shivering. It is December, then January. Winter vacation.

She has a few mornings in a row like this. Then two weeks. Dr. Davin asks her if she wants to try taking some medicine to calm her down. The idea of taking medicine terrifies her. It seems to mean she has entered a different sphere. Now she is one of them.

The idea of getting out of bed terrifies her. Or looking at the clock to see that it is only 9:04, that she has missed another day back at school—or that she hasn't missed another day of school; it is Saturday, and now the whole weekend lies ahead like a laundry chute to slide down. What if she stays like this forever? She can't let Justin see her like this. That is the only thought that gets her out of bed.

She clutches the covers to her chest, wanting to dive back into sleep, where it was safe. She wants to call out for her mother, but can't do that because Clarissa's still in bed, sleeping off last night's pink pill. Her father and Justin are out playing basketball at the local YMCA, but they will be back soon.

She tries to think of something sweet and good, so she thinks about Justin. Then she remembers; he's going that weekend on a field trip to Newton with his computer camp, and what if the bus crashes. She pictures it in her head, the bus rolling over and over, catching on fire, bursting into flames. What if Justin dies? What if she feels so bad today because he is going to die?

A little chant starts in her head. *If Justin dies, I die, if Justin dies, I die*—a nursery rhyme. Certain thoughts or phrases get stuck in her head lately, like *I have no friends,* or *Everything I do is wrong.*

But the main thing she keeps thinking is, *I can't, I can't, I can't, I can't.*

The little engine that couldn't. *Can't what?* she asks herself. But her own brain echoes back: *I . . . just . . . can't.*

Underground

It is delicious, this sleep of the dead. She doesn't dream or worry or think. Her mother calls the school and explains that her daughter is not well.

Stephanie shuffles out to watch the daytime movies, the old comedies. She likes the black-and-white ones best. Nothing with too much color. She and her mother sip tea, and sometimes Stephanie pretends to nibble a piece of toast. Getting crumbs on her lap.

Then, back to the warmth of the bed, the cool sheets, the blankets, the down comforter pulled up to her chin. Up high, outside her window, she can see snowflakes falling a long way down out of the sky, opening up like parachutes just before they land. She sleeps, the earth sleeps.

Justin sits on her bed and peers into her face. "Are you all right?" he asks, his little face making an effort to seem smooth. "You are, you know." He shows her his newest magic trick, pulls a silver coin from her ear. "I'm practicing," he says. Each day he shows her a new trick.

He brings her all of her favorite foods to tempt her.

But nothing tempts her.

Rush Hour

She and Denny have tickets to go to the Boston Philharmonic for President's Day. Which president? No one was actually born on this day who is or was president. They might as well make it White Sale Day. Television Show Day.

He bought them a month ago. She wants to tell him, *Take Kit, he's the music lover,* but she can't find a way to say it that doesn't sound sardonic.

She just wants to be at peace.

Take Kit.

Take my wife ... please.

So she goes with him to the Boston Philharmonic, and they decide to travel by train. She'll keep her hands off strange men's legs this time. But no, she can't make that joke, either. Nothing about strange men. There are so many things now they avoid talking about.

How about the Red Sox? Think they'll make it into the World Series? How about them Yankees. . . . Maybe it will snow. Maybe it will rain. Maybe it won't.

They have to get off and change trains in one of the Boston suburbs because of an engine problem. They stand around in the station of a little town that has recently won a beautification-of-America award. A brass plaque says so. It is just past five o'clock on a Friday afternoon, already dark, and men and women rush past them. White houses, red bows on the doors. Commuters streaming by like colored ribbons.

The apparition of these faces in a crowd . . .

But she cannot catch her breath. She doesn't know what is wrong with her; maybe she's having a heart attack.

Can you die of a heart attack when you're seventeen years old? She thinks it's possible, that she's read about such things happening, though it usually seems to be athletes who suddenly drop down. Her heart is pounding wildly. The commuters go by in blurs of separate arms, wrists, legs, feet.

petals on a wet, black bough . . .

This is what Ezra Pound saw, coming out of the London Underground, but for him it was an image of beauty. Stephanie is terrified. She presses back against a wall. Denny strides ahead. She watches his black wool overcoat grow smaller, blend with the crowd. The platform steams in the cold; her own breath raises a mist over her face. A train pulls in with a grinding metallic shriek.

There are voices coming from behind her head, apparently over a loudspeaker system, but she can't locate the speakers anywhere. It seems to be a conversation, but she can't make out any of the words. She crouches low to the ground, as if, should her heart literally fall out of her chest, it wouldn't have that far to fall.

A stranger pauses. "Miss? Are you all right, miss?"

She nods her head, breathing shallowly. Gasping like a fish.

This is ridiculous! But she can't get up. Another stranger pauses. This one has a sharp, long face, sharp long teeth, like a wolf. "Steph? Get up."

"I can't," she says. The words that have been boiling inside for so long. *I can't I can't I can't go on with this.*

Watching It Go

The train pulls away from the station, leaving them behind. Denny stands so tall and straight-backed, so helpless, his big black-gloved hands dangling at his sides, watching it go.

Nine O'Clock

She lies in bed and opens her eyes again to see the second hand sweep past the minute hand at exactly 9 a.m. She wakes up every single day at nine.

Why nine? Why not six o'clock or seven, or ten?

She tries to remember if anything awful ever happened at 9 a.m. Some traumatic event.

Elementary school always began at nine, from kindergarten through sixth grade. But that doesn't explain anything. For the most part, Stephanie has always liked school okay. In fact, all her life she's been a happy person; an easy baby, her mother says. That is what is so scary about this thing—paralyzed, underground, each morning at nine o'clock. Nine o'clock exactly, clockwork. She wants to wake up dead. Maybe she's already died. There is absolutely no reason for any of this; it doesn't make sense.

She thinks, I want out.

But out of what?

Waiting for Nine O'Clock

Stephanie decides to beat the demon clock, so she sets the alarm for seven a.m. Early. Maybe this way she can outwit the gods. It is worth getting up a little early to try.

It works! The morning light is spreading a pink glow over the room; the world looks fresh and new, and Stephanie feels calm, normal, this morning, for the first time in a long time. She picks up a book not due for two weeks and starts reading for her report, feeling virtuous.

But then—it happens. She starts feeling taut and anxious. Even the words on the page of the book are starting to make her nervous. She thinks, I can't read anymore. She can't go back to bed, either, though, because that would be like giving up. Her heart is hammering. Outside, ice is dripping from the eaves. And she looks over at the clock, and sure enough, it's eight forty-five, and by nine she's in a full-blown panic again, gripping the sides of the bed, wanting to call out but terrified to do so much as make a sound. She has to ride it out, like a surfer on the ocean, one wave at a time. She hangs on. She hangs on.

So What

"So what?" she could tell Denny. "So what if you're gay? Whose business is it?"

He could say, "So what if you're crazy?"

So what if we are making a mess out of our lives?

So what?

It is like Justin's favorite joke. "Guess what?" he says.

"What?"

"That's what."

"Guess what?"

"What?"

"That's what."

And what if this just goes on forever, like a plague? If she never gets any better. If the weight never lifts off her chest, if her appetite never returns, if she never feels like laughing or even smiling again, or taking her clothes off to take a shower.

Then what?

What She Found

She and Jeanette Hatch have arranged to do their art history report on surrealism together. She can't remember how such a thing happened, except that Denny must have somehow brought it about. Jeanette Hatch has never in her life gotten anything below an A, in any subject. She is even good at gym. She doesn't seem to like one subject better than any other; she works through it, like a machine, and everything comes out perfect. Her pencil drawings look like photographs. Her handwriting is like typewriting. She plays flawless clarinet in band and orchestra.

Stephanie has promised to go that afternoon to Jeanette's house to work on the report. Jeanette keeps reminding her that surrealism is a big topic.

So is realism, thinks Stephanie.

Stephanie wakes at nine, hooked in the claws of this thing the instant she opens her eyes. It's as if her brain is keeping track of time all night while she is sleeping, because she actually wakes watching the second hand sweep past the twelve, while the minute hand is straight up and the stubby hand is on the nine.

Instant dread. Add time and stir.

The house is quiet: her dad has gone to work; Justin slept over at a buddy's house. Her mother is out somewhere; her car is gone. Instead of lying there like a shipwrecked sailor hanging on to a raft, she forces herself up out of bed. She brushes her teeth and changes out of her black turtleneck and makes the bed.

She's promised Dr. Davin to take her vitamins, drink plenty of liquids. She puts on a light jacket because it's been warm for February, warm for days now, and when she steps out into the driveway, she sees what looks like a tiny baby frog, sprawled out on the blacktop.

Then she sees a head, and a beak; it is a baby bird—was a baby bird—fallen here. She looks up, and sure enough, there is a mother sparrow, fluttering around the eaves. She didn't know that birds could have babies in winter.

Stephanie swears off eating chicken right then and there, forever.

She cannot bring herself to flush the baby bird down the toilet, and if she puts it in the garbage Justin will find it.

He has a knack for tricking lost things or hidden things out of their hiding places.

She wraps the little thing in a nest of white tissues, gets one of her mother's spades out of the gardening shed, and though the earth is hard as stone most places, she finds a few inches where she can dig into the soil, and once started she can't stop. She takes off her jacket because she's sweating in the February sun.

She digs where cats and squirrels won't get at the bird, and places the white bundle in the bottom of the hole and covers it over with loose dirt. It falls through her fingers in grains the size of chocolate cake crumbs. The sweet smell of the earth rises, the first thing she's been able to enjoy in months. She and her mother have always gardened together. These are familiar gestures.

She presses the earth down gently but firmly, as if planting a tulip bulb. She knows the corny poem by Tennyson about God watching over every little sparrow that falls— they had to memorize it back in seventh grade. She's not sure who was watching this dead bird—barely a bird at all, little more than an egg. Maybe no one was watching, exactly. But she is sure it's more than a pile of feathers and flesh and bones folded up in tissue. It's as real as she is, and as much a part of something infinitely bigger than both.

Standing there leaning on the shovel with the wind blowing strands of red hair into her mouth and the sun warming the top of her head, she is sure of it.

She washes her hands at the kitchen sink and decides to take a shower, and while she's at it, she trims her hair which has grown into a long red mop, and then makes a pitcher of lemonade with lemons, sugar, water, and ice, and now hours have passed, almost a whole day, and she is much too tired to do anything. She calls Jeanette and tells her she won't be coming over.

"Why not?" Jeanette says, obviously annoyed.

"My mother won't let me," Stephanie lies. "She worries when I'm out after dark." It's almost four in the afternoon. Surely it should be getting dark soon. Yes, at the horizon the winter sky is turning a foiled silver-silver gray. She breathes a sigh of relief. The long day is almost over; she has survived another. "My mom worries a lot."

"Oh," Jeanette says. There's a pause. Stephanie wonders if Denny has told her something about her mother. "I've been working on Federico Garcia Lorca," she tells Stephanie. "I'm just about done with him. So you should pick someone else, okay?" She sounds like an exasperated adult. Stephanie wonders if Jeanette Hatch has ever been a child. "Why don't you try Salvadore Dalí?" Jeanette suggests.

Stephanie is in no position to argue, and they get off the phone but she's thinking, isn't Salvadore Dalí the one with the melting clocks? And the flies crawling over them?

Isn't he the guy who signed blank canvases and had other people paint the pictures, hundreds of them, and sold them for a bunch of cash? She thinks that's pretty surreal.

First Flower

A hyacinth pushes its purple head up out of the dirt, the grayish-brown color of refrigerated chocolate. The blossoms still clenched tight, in violet stars, and birds singing like mad in the suddenly mild air, and warmth spreading on one side of her face in one full minute of sun, and half a minute of peace.

The Other Mouth

Ben's mouth fascinates her. It looks so full and heavy, sulky. She keeps thinking about how thick his tongue must be, and how it would feel moving in her mouth, kissing her. She tries not to look at his lips when they sit together talking; she looks at the beige carpeting, at the library books till he says, "Hey, yoohoo! You still with me, here?" or lets a book drop with a thud onto the library table. "I just wanted to make sure you were awake."

She doesn't see how such a gentle voice can come out of such a gangster mouth.

Safe

You can feel safe with something that stifles you. You can feel safer not breathing, not moving, holding still, playing dead.

But you can only do it for so long.

Happy New Year

She has been avoiding him for weeks, but at the end of February, Denny says he has something he wants to tell her. Even though she's been waiting for this phone call, expecting it, praying for it, dreading it, she's amazed at the way her stomach drops to what feels like her knees.

She hoists it back up and says, "Okay."

When her mother drops her off at his house, she tells her to come back in half an hour.

"Half an hour? That's all?"

"That's all it will take," she says.

He holds her hand tightly in his. She looks at their linked fingers with what already feels like nostalgia. As if she is looking at them from a long way off. This moment won't come again. This holding.

"It's okay," she says. "Really."

When they come to it, neither one knows exactly what to say. There is a question in his blue eyes, and an answer in hers; they lean against each other, shoulder to shoulder.

She looks at his photos from Jamaica, but really she is trying to memorize his face. It won't be *her* face anymore.

He says, "I'll call you." Her mother honks out in the driveway. "We'll talk soon." She runs out lightly, as if someone had given her back her girlhood.

Justin opens the car door for her, sees something in her look and grins. "Welcome back."

Afterward

A spirit of peace descends. The ax, once fallen, loses its sharpness. Loses its terror.

She and Justin play Chutes and Ladders, and Candyland. Her father joins them. Her mother suggests a game of cards.

The house feels ordinary and light.

It is February, the shortest month of winter, and the light lasts a little longer, each day, day by day.

Progress

Dr. Davin says she is making progress. She moves from three blue antianxiety pills to two, then to three yellow, then two, then one. She takes Neurontin three times a day to control her mood swings, and an antidepressant shaped like a small blue boat.

Her closet used to look empty, because everything inside was black. Now she hangs a light blue blouse, a pair of green velvet pants. New clothes, new sizes. She and Diane go shopping.

They are already showing bathing suits in the department stores.

She has lost twelve pounds since the fall. For a while it was twenty. She has gone from looking like a fourteen-year-old to looking like a gray emaciated twelve-year-old ghost, and is now edging her way back toward adolescence. She eats grapefruit for breakfast, a protein shake for lunch, and whatever her mother serves for dinner. Tiny portions. Small bites.

Ever since finding the dead baby bird, she has been vegetarian. She likes best the taste of plain iceberg lettuce, its clean no-taste. But she tries to adds a few more foods each week: yams, broccoli, succotash, lentil soup. Her mother hums at the sink, scrubbing vegetables.

She has her daughter back.

Spring

Ben asks her to the movies. Neither one mentions Denny. Surprisingly, Ben invites Justin along. Justin is thrilled. This is his first date.

They decide to go to some kids' comedy that is playing at the newest movie theater. Because the multiplex is new, the seats are still comfortable, the heat works, and the cup holders still hold the cups. Ben buys Justin two kinds of candy and fruit punch. Justin flies off with his ticket stub between his teeth to claim the best seats and hold them. Ben buys a giant-size popcorn and a giant-size drink, and just when she thinks he's going to ask if she wants anything, too, he gestures with the huge containers and says, "These are for you."

She could not eat that much popcorn or drink that much lemonade if he gave her six months to do it, but she doesn't object. There is something almost springlike in the damp March air today. Stephanie is wearing a flowered scarf—not to get dressed up for a date, just because, for the first time in months, she feels like wearing something soft and bright again, something ... pretty.

Once they are in their seats—Stephanie in the middle—she can smell Ben's men's cologne, the inexpensive kind you buy in a drugstore, like English Leather or Brut. It mixes with the smell of soap and the little-boy scent of Justin's hair, and the overwhelming buttery smell of the popcorn. The red velvet curtains.

A third of the way into the movie, in the safe velvety dream-dark of the theater, Justin hands Stephanie one kernel of popcorn. She eats it without thinking. Puts her hand out for another. He hands her one more. Finally, after he's done this five or six times, she starts eating the popcorn by the handful, just like everybody else, as if she's been doing it all her life. As if she's always belonged in the land of the living.

Ben takes her other hand.

It's a matinee, but the safe dark of the movie theater seems like the only real time or place or temperature in the world. In another hour or two, they will all walk outside into sunlight. The grass is starting to come up green again where all winter it lay matted and brown. And night will come a little later each day till midsummer, and then it will turn, and begin wheeling unevenly again toward fall and winter.

Like birds flying and landing, pausing and pushing forward, flying south and coming home, fleeing and returning, heading off again into the unknown, changing direction. The clock, the calendar, the lopsided earth itself. And so it goes like that, on and on and on.